VŨ PHAN

12 SHORT STORIES OF WIND'S MEMORIES

NHÂN ẢNH 2024

12 SHORT STORIES OF WIND'S MEMORIES
Author: Vũ Phan
Cover: Uyên Nguyên Trần Triết
Layout: Huỳnh Hoa
Editor: Lê Hân
Nhân Ảnh Publisher 2024
ISBN: 979-8-8693-1269-3

TABLE OF CONTENT

Black Tears Forest	7
Silverado Moonlight	21
Star Gathering Season In "Cao Thach" Village	43
Tan's Little Snake	59
The Deadly Blow	83
The Funeral Man Mours The Sea	103
The Grean Meadow And Sunny Summer	115
The Last Trip Of The Old Fisherman	135
The Man Who Saw The Angel	161
The Sweet Potato Islet	175
The Thief From "That Son" Mountains	203
The Town Without Coffe Shops	241

BLACK TEARS FOREST

The rain kept falling relentlessly as there was a giant lake hanging above the village. For more than a week, the sky has been filled with soggy gray clouds. To the residents of the village sitting on the hillside near the Truong Son range, this scene was too familiar. Every year from September, tropical storms regularly came visiting them like a close friend. They then disappeared in late December when a cold northeast wind blew southwards.

Standing on the porch of his house sitting on the low hill at the beginning of the village road, Mr. Mau watched the rain that falling from noon, now still pouring down. He then dressed in a raincoat, handled hoe, and walked down to the field.

The deserted road at the foothill likely was just him. The desolate scene covering the rooftops, gardens, and fields spreads far to the west. For over a hundred years, houses in this village have often been built at the foothill that blocked the path to the high plateau. On their sides was a vast old forest.

Born and raised here, Mr. Mau had been told an old story as most villagers did. According to the tale of old ancestors, when the first people came here to exploit the wild land, they had seen big tall trees living on the rocks next to deep, treacherous creeks in the forest. They were shielded by thick layers of green bushes, and cold water springs winding and then pouring into large streams flowing through the village. When evening down, moisture evaporates and gathers into dew clang on mossy branches and canopies.

Every year, during the rainy season, the forest was even more tranquil and colder. Rainwaters were similar crystal beads, falling through that darkness that made them look like black tears. The first people who came here to cut wood and hunt saw those strange blackish raindrops. When returning to the village, they had named the forest Hac Le – Black Forest.

Many generations have passed, and people here still call the old forest on the western hillsides by the weird name Hac Le. The village's descendants who have passed away always advise their children and grandchildren not to harm this mysterious forest. They said Hac Le was rich and contained abundant resources, and provisions. Anyone could go hunting, and gathering to earn life or make some money. Only one thing, villagers absolutely must not cut down old trees. According to them, there were forest gods who guarded the disasters that would come from the west, and protect their village. The day these old trees no longer exist, the heavy rains will transform into harsh flash floods that will soon wreak havoc on men and property. Once the water vanishes, then the fields will be dried up. A tragic story of the dead still haunted most of the villagers. It told about the disaster that happened more than half a century ago, that still terrified the old people. That year, summer was really hot and extremely dry. At the end of the dry season, the streams were only bare rocks exposed to the rude sun. All villagers depended on the wells dug into the deep ground. Hunger due to poor harvests, everyday villagers had flocked to Hac Le forest to pick vegetables and edible tubers and set traps.

While being careless, some villagers built a cooking fire, the daring flame quickly spreading to the dead leaves. Unfortunately, at the same moment, raging winds from the west fueled more dry air, the big fire bursting and overwhelming the whole forest. For several days, it had burned down countless old trees.

As the fire had gone, the whole village looked anxiously to the smoky forest on the hillside now just bare rocks and fallen trunks.

During the rainy season that year, soil and rocks from above the village were swept away by floodwaters, then filling fields, gardens, creeks, and roads. Then disasters constantly struck one after another. Many families had to leave their homes, fields, and gardens to elsewhere. The rest had suffered calamity and poverty for years.

Nearly ten years later, the dead forest had recovered its lush green. People have been called to return. Witnessing that horrible disaster, the villagers have met together. They decided to protect the forest and the old trees liked their eyes.

Mr. Mau remembers the day the war ended, luckily their forest was still intact on the hillside, exposing its green canopies. Many villagers ran away to hide from war, and now returned to their homes and started a new life. Remembering the words of their predecessors, they went into the forest to cut down small trees to build houses and collected dry firewood. Not to down the old trees. Gardens and fields have been cared for by good men, gradually becoming green. Years went by, and more and more people returned. The village grew bigger, new houses being built.

People certainly thought peace would come and life would be filled with laughs and wealth. But unpredictably, post-war times were so hard. Poverty and famine had covered the whole village. Villagers were desperate for cooperatives way. They evaded working in the fields, only yielding enough food to make their families survive.

At a dead end, everyone went to Hac Le forest to find something to eat. During those desperate times, many of them defied the old advice, went exploited the old forest.

Despite mindless thinking, no one dared to give the first axes to down the trees. When the elders heard the news, they stopped the idea of exploiting the forest. The tall trees were saved again.

oOo

Twenty years later, Mr. Mau was still a farmer. But his hair and beard got gray. The village was now crowded. It was quite different from the past years. A large road runs from the coastal town to his village and then connects to the forest trails. Electric poles appearing along roads. They brought city light to his village and drove the darkness away. More and more people and vehicles went from other towns to do business in his village.

Exiled peoples, now have brought back a hastening lifestyle. Right in the center of the village, there were a lot of busy shops that he had never seen before in his life. The highland village now looked like a small town. Young people changing more than he could imagine. Sinking into the money fever, they traded all kinds of goods. The whole village was haunted by wealth and luxurious goods. Some villagers instantly got rich. People began talking and pursuing the lifestyle in big cities. The calm countryside air was faded.

Every time, when he passed by the market, Mr. Mau felt like a stranger. One time, he met his pre-wartime classmate. They two walked to a store next to the bridge crossing the stream by the noisy shops. Sitting next to a small table with a spirits bottle and a fried peanut dish. When he tried it, he found its taste not as good as the old one. Chewing some roasted peanuts, they were not as crunchy and delicious as those grown in the village fields. In a moment, he realized the good old things probably had gone. Just the old stories remained, making his heart burst with joy and sadness. They excitedly talked about the garden, fields, and another old mate. Some had gone abroad, and some still making friends with farming. Some are missing to nowhere.

The thing that connected him with his old friend was the forest. He thought it was the most valuable property that the village elders would leave for the next generations. After he dried up the bottle, he called the middle-aged fat man to charge. After a few greeting words, Mr. Mau randomly found that they were also old neighbors. The generous man brought another bottle of good wine to serve. Meeting an old neighbor, he revealed some bad news that was stalking the villagers. This was a story that some people went into the forest to seek timber for new houses. They saw forest poachers chop down tall trees and then traded with sawmills for money. Hac Le forest once more was threatened by deforesters and traders. After some successful businesses, the bad guys have found that the village forest was a treasure. So they incited villagers with lucrative contracts. Men whisper that those guys also build other hidden roads running to the south foothills, by passing the villagers' eyes. The shop owner was a disappointed story to let Mr. Mau down. The villain's greed drove people to ruin nature and destroy Hac Le forest.

When saying goodbye to his old classmate, he looked at him and said:
"Perhaps when we die, there won't be any wood left in the forest to make a coffin to bury us."

Standing hesitantly by the bridge, Mr. Mau remembered the old days.

At the time when the stream was still clear, village youngsters often came to swim and fish on summer days. Now the new market has dumped trash there, floating here and there on the stream and then stuck on the rocks along the bank, drawing a dirty scene.

Since the day he met his old friend, every morning before going down to the field at the foothill, Mr. Mau stood on the porch looking at Hac Le forest appearing under dim light in the distant hill range. He wanted to see how it changed overnight in the dark. Its quiet appearance seemed to hide the camps, the lumberjacks, and the sharp axes were buried under the dense canopy of dark green leaves. He imagined that one day the forest would be finished. Its death will be the death knell for this village.

Bad news from Hac Le forest has burst as a big firecracker. Villagers secretly discovered that tall trees had been cut down. When some people have been there, only the dead stumps remain on the hillside.

Mr. Mau quit his work. He and an old neighbor walk there. The forest was dissected by zig-zag paths, now were exposed to the sunlight. Lumbermen's truck wheels have plowed everywhere, and a horrified scene appeared on the hillsides, so far only the lush green existed. Without some local men's help, the bad guys from other towns dare not do this, Mr. Mau thought. Some camps of lumbermen were not far from his sight. He and his neighbor witnessed the ravage with sad eyes. However, the whole village kept silent. Life still continued with doubt. Nobody had been arrested.

Mr. Mau and his old friend have missed the forest. They seemed very worried. The villager no longer respects the advice of the elders. Many people in his village became instantly rich after one night. The market was noisier like a coastal town. People saw more big houses being built with more vehicles on the roads, drastically changing the face of the countryside in the highlands.

The hillsides above the village had been covered with trees for long years, now exposed to sunlight. People didn't know what to do with bare land. Some villagers tried growing some crops there. But the steep, jagged stones could not retain the fertile humus layer, so they failed. The lovely streams gradually lost their vitality and turned into dry gullies.

Mr. Mau felt sad. He worried about the fields at the foothills. After some years, crops would no longer be able to grow here. Disaster appeared during the rainy season. Rocks and soil poured down from the hillsides to the edge of the village, gradually burying fields, gardens, and roads around the market. The large stream flowed under the bridge, turning a small creek weaving through gravel in the summer. But suddenly submerged by flash floods rushing from the hills, then overflowing and crashing houses and people on its bank. Other streams running through gardens and fields have suffered the same fate.

The fierce floods swept away everything on its way down to the seashores. Sometimes, people and livestock were injured or killed, and houses and crops were damaged. After heavy rains, villagers have to work hard to clear dirt and rocks to save fields and gardens from being choked.

People now feared the rainy season. They recalled the horrible disaster that happened some decades ago. In the dark time the old trees in Hac Le forest no longer bear the black tears on the hillsides, the disasters will not spare the village.

Mr. Mau's melancholy thought about his old age. Maybe someday, he would have to leave this village and be exiled again. But he and his long-time friend probably are not willing to leave. They would stay here and witness the death of Hac Le forest and their old house./.

SILVERADO MOON LIGHT

Annaheim's atmosphere was quite boring. Khan N. put a handbag in his car and then drove to Silverado, Santa Ana mountains. Yesterday, he had made a call in advance to Kevin, a good friend of his. This guy was the owner of a nice house in that mountainous land.

Kevin said I must go to San Francisco for business. The time returned to Silverado was unknown. The key was hidden in the garden and enjoyed while being in Silverado.

Having been in Kevin's house several times, Khan N. has loved the quiet air and forest, hills, and streams there when he would like to escape the noisy city.

Khan Nguyen arrived in Silverado at noon. The mountains and forests were tranquil under summer light. He parked his car in the shade, then stepped out to watch the nice landscape on the hill slope for some minutes. Then walking to the garage, I found the hidden key under a log near a bush.

Khan Nguyen opened the front door, relaxing on the wooden step, listening light breeze blowing through branches, wild birds singing in the air, and watching sparse trees lining up on the roadside. In front of the house, a low fence was built with gray stone slabs that were stacked layer by layer and then strengthened with grout.

Kevin has told Khan N. the story of his house. The ex-owner was an old retired army architect. That man had renovated everything as his will after possessing it. Then after, he and his wife have lived here for many years. The poor old man only returned to their ex-house in Orange after his beloved wife passed away. Maybe he tried fleeing the loneliness.

After resting for a few minutes on the porch, Khai picked up his bag and walked to the kitchen. He felt hungry now. Sitting in a chair by the table, Khan N. had a hamburger left after breakfast in a paper bag and ate it. Looking at a beer bottle in the refrigerator, he found so many things inside that a strong guy couldn't consume in a single week. Khan opened the window for some fresh air. Outside, in the backyard, bright sunlight danced on the flowers and grasses. I went up a bit further, and there was a winding trail creeping into a thin forest. Ideal for people who love hiking through nice hills.

His cell phone just broke the quiet air. The soft tones filled the kitchen room. Khan N. watched the fresh message. Hoang Le, his girlfriend in Viet Nam has sent a few photos captured the rain storm falling on the hills outside the hospital window, then her comments about the weather in Bao Loc town, in Lam Dong plateau. The heavy storm overwhelmed the misty hills and mountains in the early morning and looked dull and lonely. He took some photos of the summer scene in Silverado under sunshine that spread around the garden, then sent them back to her.

Late afternoon, when the sun went down in the west, he locked the door and walked out of the house. The air was fresher along the hills. Khan N. walking towards the far forest in the north. Familiar scenes were appearing on roadsides where he and Kevin had been here last February. Today the sky was clear and shining. The cold, misty days of late winter were gone. Some lone houses sit between tree wood next to a trail. Khan N. recalled the roads winding among green orchards, farms, and creeks … in Bao Loc highland, Vietnam.

After walking for more than half an hour, he relaxed and sat down on a dry grass bed along the road, took off his sunglasses and hat, and drank some water. A few minutes later, an Asian girl sitting behind the wheel of a white Jeep drove by. Khan N. watched the off-road car with an opening sunroof moving with little noise on an empty road. In a moment, the girl tilted her head and glanced at him. He loved that sturdy car that likely be built for mountain rough roads. The girl and the white car were moving away and disappeared. The dead leaves were tossed into the air then rolling after the wind.

Relaxing for a while, he started another walk in thirty minutes. Then left the main road and moved towards another trail running to the fields. The sun was now like a small red ball hiding in the clouds. He stopped under a canopy, the trail here radiating in smaller paths crossing deeper the Santa Ana range.

This afternoon, just him in the hill area, Khan N. hiked through the way that he had passed. The sun was going down in the west. Khan N. finished the last road stretch over the hillside and then went down the slope towards Kevin's house backyard. He took some deep breaths and washed his face under the fountain. Cool air gave more freshness. He walked on the path on the right wing to bypass the house towards the front yard.

Khan N. sat on the bench under the veranda, watching the sun getting lower over the distant cities along the coast. The long hiking outdoors made him feel alert. His body got rid of the lethargy he had suffered since coming back from Vietnam. From the far side of the road, the engine sounds echo in the calm space. The white Jeep was running in the fading light. The sunroof was still open for the air and the wind blew out the girl's hair. While the car passed in front of the house, she was looking at him with her nice brown eyes. This time she caught Khan N.'s attention. He had been here several times, but never seen her and her car..

Moments later, he was even more surprised when the white Jeep appeared across the road. The light on the left side turned on, and the car wheels rolled through the gate and parked next to his. Khai still sat quietly on the bank. The girl with shoulder-length black hair, and a symmetrical, nice face opened the car door, got out then approached him, and greeted:
-Hi, you are the owner of this house?
 Hearing her question in Vietnamese. Khan N. smiled and replied:

-No, this is my friend's house. I guess, you are Vietnamese?

-Yes, that's right. Driving by and seeing you, I thought you were a newcomer to this area. Last time I met a white man wearing glasses sitting on a bench. So he's your friend?

Khan N. nodded:

-Right. I'm living in Anaheim. I just came here at noon. And will stay for a couple of days. Maybe when you passed by, then guess whether I was Vietnamese?

The girl smiled with shyness, and looked into his eyes:

-I guess so, luckily I'm right

They both laughed. Her beautiful brown eyes turned to the small garden. He actively extended his hand to the strange girl:

-My name is Khan N.

-My name is Jenny Ha

-There's only one bench out here, please sit

-Yes, thank you

Jenny Ha naturally sat down, and made a short distance from him:

-Ms. Ha's house nearby?

-About five miles from here. Seemingly, I have seen you while you were sitting on the roadside, right?

-Yes, I like to hike around this mountainous area every time I have been here. Kevin, the house owner just went to San Francisco this morning. How long have you been in Silverado?

-No, I am living in another place

-I've been here a few times before, but I didn't see you... Oh, sorry I will bring you some drink

Khai stood up. He intended to walk into the house. Said the girl:

-Thank you, I got water in the car

She went to the Jeep and got a water bottle then turned back:

-My home is in Orange. I only come here when having some day off

-Oh, yes. Miss Ha had a beautiful car

Hearing his compliment, Ha looked a little bit shy her cheeks went light pink. She was watching the car parking next to the garage and said:

-Yes, this one is quite old. Grandfather gave it to me

Leaving the story unfinished, they two looked at the red sunlight reflecting on the far faint clouds in the west. The late sundown scenery was glorious. Khai asked:

-When you were in Vietnam, your family lived in Saigon or somewhere?

-My parents' home is near Phan Rang town. And where's your home?

-My family was in Bao Loc town, Lam Dong. The whole family has been here for a long time, almost ten years. Likely you have minded to this house?

-Yes, I loved it

Khai was surprised to hear she spoke. He said:

-Oh, really... me too. I have heard my friend say, the previous owner was an architect. He built this house by himself. It looks nice in this mountainous region

She turned her head to the right and looked through the window glass to the living room inside. Then looked at him and asked:

-Could I get in and see inside?

-Yes, of course

Khan N. stood up, opened the door then led her in. She walked on the wooden floor to the gray stone fireplace, looking at the wooden squirrel carved from a pine log. Then gently touched the brown wood lid of the old piano that looked like an antique with her sweet eyes. Khan N. has been here many times, but occasionally, he saw Kevin sitting on the short bench, playing some country song in the evening. Leaving the girl alone, Khai went to the kitchen to get some water. When he turned back, she had walked out and sitting motionless under the veranda. Seeing him step out the door, she stood up and said:

-I have to go home

Khan N. felt a bit strange. He thought she would stay longer. She steps towards the Jeep. Khai was behind, but he quickly moved forward to open the car door. She said:

-Thank you

She raised her hand and said goodbye to him. The Jeep slowly steered towards the gate, then turned right and sped away.

After dinner, Khan N. sat alone on the bench under the soft yellow light of the lamp hanging next to the door. His cell phone just rang. Khan N. turned it on. Hoang Le, his girlfriend sent new pictures of pitied Montagnard patients who defied the bad weather, they brought their children to her hospital. She expressed her love for these poor people:

"I loved these Ba Na patients, they are so gentle and lovely. Most of them live in high mountains far from the town. Once upon a time, an old woman brought some chicken eggs in a basket and walked from morning till noon to the hospital and gave them to me. The whole village was Christian and loved God very much."

Khai smiled himself. He remembered when they studied together in high school, Hoang Le was a student who loved nature, flowers and small birds, butterflies, and cats. These little creatures sometimes appeared in dense bushes around their homes.

oOo

A day of wandering on the trails in the Santa Ana mountains lasted until the afternoon before Khan N.

returned home. After dinner, he turned on the light at the door and sat in the living room listening to music. Khan N. looked at the piano and the wooden squirrel on the fireplace. Yesterday when she had been here, Jenny Ha seemed to love these wooden things.

Khan N. has been in Silverado for some days. The day after tomorrow, he had to drive back to Anaheim.

Daily hiking in the morning or late afternoon, he's not seen Jenny Ha's Jeep yet on the road. He guessed, maybe she had moved back to Orange.

Khan N. was reading a fiction book in the living room. This was his most preferred time besides a hiking moment in the woods. The sudden car sound bursting from the dark outside. The shining light from the road reached the front yard. The calmness was broken. Khan N. opened the door and walked under the veranda. Jenny Ha appeared with a square box in her hand. Within the twilight of the evening, her face looked so gentle.

-Hello – he smiled

-Hello, have you dinned already?

-Yes, done. The whole day walking on the trails made my hunger so big

She laughed to hear his humor. His hand gently held the paper box.

-I bringing along some cakes I just baked

-Thank Jenny Ha. Do you like to stay outside for fresh air?

-Yeap

He put the box on the bench and then asked:

-Coffee or tea?

-Coffee

    Khai walked into the kitchen, then made two coffee cups and brought them outside. The tranquil night overwhelmed the hills and trees. Few ocean breezes blew gently, dissipating heat still lurking in the darkness. Jenny Ha handed the coffee cup while listening to the music from the living room. She smiled and asked:

-The music is great. Do you love Vietnamese or American music?

He put down the cup on the chair:

-Vietnamese music, also the music here... And what music do you love?

-After coming here, I still loved Vietnamese songs. Do you like to listen to the piano?

Khai noded:

-Yes, sometimes. Could you play piano, right?

-Yes, first years when my family was here, I started studying piano at home. In Orange, my grandfather has given me one

She opened the box's lid, took out a round cake with brown chocolate crust, and then handed it to him.

-Thank

He tried and smelled the nice vanilla scent:

-You're so skillful. The cake is delicious

-In Vietnam, I studied cooking and baking with my mum

She finished the cake while drinking some coffee. In a silent moment, Jenny Ha watched the trees standing dimly in the dark of the garden. He thought she was probably thinking of someone. Her voice was gentle:

-I loved this place. This house reminded my grandfather who had lived here quite a long, before sold it to other people

What she just revealed surprised Khai. He saw her eyes seemingly searching somewhere into the darkness that covered the road in front of the house.

-Oh, so the architect, ex-owner is your grandfather?

-Yes, my grandfather was an army engineer who went to Vietnam in wartime. His post is located near his grandmother's home. They often met on the road and they fell in love. When grandmother was pregnant, grandfather was injured in a battle. So, he had to return to the USA. Grandfather had written a note and asked the help from a Vietnamese soldier to leave that message to Grandmother. He had said, that he would come back to marry her. But for unknown reasons, he could not come back to Vietnam again. Grandma waited in the village and gave birth to my mother

The story begins as a nice novel about love during war. It made Khan N. try to imagine what happened to them. She briefly looked into Khan N.'s eyes and continued:

-After the war ended, my grandmother had to raise my mother alone. Wait so long, she then married another man and had two more children

-Grandpa won't return to Vietnam?

A bit sad, she replied:

-Yeah. Grandfather was demobilized and went to university. Then he married his American wife here

-Jenny Ha, you were born in Vietnam?

-Yes, my mother lived in Phan Rang with her grandparents. Then she grew up, got married, and gave birth to me and two brothers. Almost ten years later, my grandfather suddenly came back to Vietnam. He returned to Phan Rang to look for my grandmother and my mom. Grandfather said, now he was a construction contractor and had many houses in California. So he wanted to take everyone to his hometown. But grandmother stayed with her Vietnamese grandfather. My parents brought the whole family here. Living in my grandfather's house in Orange until now.

Khai leaned back against the bench behind him. He heard that Jenny Ha always politely called her grandfather's new wife a real grandmother.

-You told a great story. So you ever lived in this house?

-No, because the house was sold after my grandmother passed away. I have seen pictures that my grandfather had taken every corner. There was a photo of grandparents taken next to the fireplace and a wooden squirrel statue sat on the piano. My grandfather met my grandmother in Vietnam. She was a Buddhist. So he believed in Buddhism since then. Though he was Christian here. After his grandmother passed away, he told me that he often saw her spirit walking around the living room and kitchen

-How about the house in Silverado that Ha is living in now?

-My grandparents here have two sons. One went working in Texas, the other was in the army. Now grandfather has passed away too. But he rarely came to this house when he was still alive. Only me. Sometimes, my father drove my mother here to relax in the summer

Sitting silently for a while, Khan N. asked:

-Would you play some Vietnamese music

-Yes, if you like

She was walking into the living room. Khai sat outside listening to the melodious notes from the old piano. Sometimes the sounds drifting gently like sad, lamenting night winds. Khan N. imagined Jenny Ha's long fingers moving over the old piano keys. He heard familiar music and tried to remember. But his memory was empty. After playing some romantic songs, she returned to the bench, ate cake, and drank coffee.

- Jenny Ha plays very well. Unfortunately, I don't remember those songs. I guess it was composed before 1975, right?

-Yes, by musician Truong Sa, a Navy officer. My father loved listening to them when I played piano. Me too

-During the war, your father was probably a soldier.

-Yes, he was a Navy serviceman. When the Vietnam War ended, he was still young. What does your father do in Vietnam?

-My father was a teacher. Grandfather was a soldier of the Republic of Vietnam

-Do you often return to Vietnam?

-I just came back to visit my uncle living in Bao Loc and my high school girlfriend. Now she is a doctor at the town hospital. Recently, my girlfriend was just granted a scholarship from a university in Washington state. Shortly, she'll go to Seattle to study for two years.

She smiled, slightly retracted her shoulders, and said:

-Your girlfriend is a good doctor

Khai kept silent for a moment then asked:

-Do you often hiking here?

-Yes, sometimes

- OK, I will come to see you tomorrow. We'll hike together through the woods

-Yes, I am still here for two more days

She stood up. Her brown eyes calmly watching the night sky and the moon:

-I go home now. See you tomorrow morning

Khai glanced at his watch:

-Do you need me to take you home?

-No need. I would drive home alone. Thank
They walked side by side to the Jeep. Khai opened the car's door:
-Good night
She sat behind the wheel and said:
-Good night

In the quiet dark, the engine sound broke the night. The car turned on the lights and moved towards the gate, then steering to the empty road, its dim red lights gradually disappeared. Khan N. was still sitting on the bench. Only the moonlight gently shining the garden and the stone fence.

After midnight, Khan N. was awakened by some strange noise in the kitchen. Looking at the clock, it was only 2 a.m. He wondered may someone walking in the living room or a thief had broken into the house. He slowly opened the door. Kevin was sitting next to a wine bottle, eating the cakes in the box. He asked:
-The cake is so delicious. Did you buy that?
-No, the old landlord's niece brought them here

Khai walked over and sat on the nearby chair, drinking some water. Kevin looked at him with surprise:

-So, she is your friend. When did she get here?

Seeing his wide eyes behind white glasses under long, messy hair, Khai smiled:

-No, her name is Jenny Ha, a Vietnamese girl, living a few miles from here. She drove by and saw me sitting in the front yard. Then she got in and talked with me

Kevin said with astonishment:

-Oh, a Vietnamese girl. That is strange. The old owner of this house is Mexican

-Ok, Jenny Ha said he was a US officer who went to the Vietnam War and fell in love with her grandmother over there

He sipped some wine, then nodded his head a few times and said:

-The story she told you seemed so long. Now I understood... Did she play piano? I see the piano lid was opened.

-Yes, she plays very well... She also said, her grandfather still saw the spirit of his wife in the kitchen or some time sat next to the piano in the living room.

-Oh, will she come here again?

- I don't know, maybe she will

Khan N. stood up and walked to the window. He looked out the backyard. The bright moon shed a silvery white color amid the tranquil space in the garden. He thought a beautiful moon night could wake up the souls of the dead. And sometimes they would go back to their sweet home too./.

STAR GATHERING SEASON IN "CAO THACH" VILLAGE

For generations, people have watched the clear Tinh Tu river winding its way through Cao Thach village on the left bank of the arid midland, then went down the plain towards the sea. Born and raised here, little boy, Toat has loved the summer season. He could freely run and play in the fields next to the buffaloes. In the afternoon, under the soft sunny sky, Toat brought the whole herd to graze near the river bank. Sometimes he swam in the calm stream of the river as it didn't want to leave the quiet sceneries on both banks. Toat has loved his small village tale. He's heard the old men say that Cao Thach has a long mysterious history. Most of them were vocal stories passed down through generations. No people wrote them down. So, no one knew the village's ancestors' names or where they came from. But according to a tale, one of them was a very keen man in astrology and geography. The Cao Thach's name has been given from the birthday of this village. That is also the name of the round gray stone as big as a three-room house sitting on a hilltop near the Tinh Tu river bank. People in his village were proud whenever they talked to friends or strangers about the origin of the rock. They said that generations of ancestors have thought it was a shooting star falling from the high sky to Earth. And warned their descendants not to harm this sacred place.

Also from this myth, the last week of April every year was star harvesting season in the village. Growing up among secrets, Toat couldn't hide his curiosity that always wiggling in his head. At night, sometimes standing in the yard, he looked up to big and small stars sparkling in the faraway dark sky.

It's already April. Little Toat thought, this year he would be a star picker in that last week. Last traditional

New Year, he was only 14 years old. But no one talked about the age at which a body could join the star harvesting season. The first thing Toat had to make was a large kite that could fly high in the sky. Next, he must have a very long and strong jute string to keep the kite from being blown away by strong winds. The last secret that Toat wanted to know that no one has revealed yet. People have used something tied to their kites to pick sparkling stars in the night. His query yet didn't get the answer. He did not dare to ask some adults in the village, due to fear of exposing his will or being scolded.

But little smart Toat has his way. He recalled Cung, his friend with a round, bright face and funny smile. In the village, many people had rumored that Cung's uncle once successfully picked a star.

But he was not a talkative man and didn't reveal it to anyone. To get that secret, Toat had to ask Cung. He knew Cung liked fancy items that few people owned. Just a small warbler, a long-finned fish in the stream, or a flute does not move him. Toat thought he had to take the risk.

On the upper stream of the Tinh Tu River, there was a big deep hole. Villagers said long ago, a star flew through the night sky and crashed into the hill beside the river. A star's fragment that had burstled and stuck into the river bed, created a hole. This hole was very deep, few people dared to swim there. But when the river dried up in the summer, a few brave men who had dived in to explore. They found beautiful colored stones at the bottom.

One afternoon, Toat went to the upper of the river. He carefully tied the buffalo pair to a tree after watching both banks. Toat took off his clothes and swam to the middle of the waterway. He dived into the clear and calm water. Down there, sunlight shone on the mossy rocks. Reaching the bottom, Toat felt a sharp pain in his ears, the air that had filled his chest now quickly depleted. He swiftly emerged to breathe some new one. A few minutes later, took some more deep breaths, and he dived again.

At the bottom, Toat has endured pain bravely and widened his eyes to search. He was lucky to find three colored pebbles sat next together in a hole. After swimming back to the bank, Toat curiously opened his hand to look at them. They all have round shapes as were carved by skilled craftsmen and have strange glossy white, gray, and brown colors.

The next afternoon, Toat induced Cung to the field where his buffaloes were grazing alone. He showed the pebbles that had been found at the bottom of the river. Seeing three strange colorful stones with his own eyes, Cung was still suspicious and questioned where Toat had gotten these nice things. Toat boldly pointed to the upstream of the river and firmly said that he had dived down there. After his best friend had been convinced, Toat left them all in front of Cung. He just needs help. He wanted Cung to ask his uncle how to make a kite if he wanted to pick a star. Pondering over a moment, Cung hesitately promised to help. Then picked up the whole pebbles, joyfully jumped up, and left.

By the end of the week, Toat has waited. He still didn't see Cung went to the river bank. He waited but eventually ran out of patience. So he walked to Cung's house a few times. Nevertheless, only met Cung's grandmother. Without words, she pointed towards the fields downstream of the river. But Toat couldn't leave the buffaloes grazing on the hill without watching, so he had to turn back.

Finally, Cung came to see Toat on a bright sunny afternoon on the green field. Cung frowned and said his uncle hadn't come back from town yet. Toat felt likely he didn't dare to ask or was scolded for being so curious. In return, Cung said he would give Toat some old jute string that his uncle no longer used. Toat was overjoyed by what Cung promised to give him. He knew that villagers often braided jute rope tightly into a string. Then made them into a roll and tied them to the kite. Thanks to that, the kite would fly very high in the wind. Cung said honestly then stood up and left. Sitting alone, Toat looked up at the blue sky across the river and dreamed of touching a star someday.

The traditional tale didn't reveal what people did after they had a star. Mostly people would hide it with faith that stars will bring wealth and good luck. For Toat, he only wanted to pick up a star to watch its marvelous beauty and as a favorite toy.

In the last week of April, Toat started making kites and collecting jute string that was scattered everywhere in the village. This month, villagers were spinning jute fibers and drying them in the fields before selling them in the market. While the buffalo herd patiently grazed, Toat spent their free time making kites. Then braiding short pieces of jute into a long, sturdy string. Cao Thach jutes grown on the riverbank were famed for their durability throughout the region.

Everything was done. He just waited for Cung each afternoon. Out in the fields, the wind rustled in the air, inviting kites to fly high into the sky.

Keeping the promise, Cung brought Toat a roll of jute string. He was despaired and told that he had done all things he could. But his uncle said nothing about how to pick a star. Couldn't ask more, Toat had to forget and try to find another way. Remembered when playing around the fields, he and his friends tried to catch dragonflies hovering over grasses. They used to rub jackfruit sap on the stick. Then tired dragonflies' wings landed there, their legs were stuck in and couldn't escape.

Inside Toat's imaginative little head, he has hoped a star would less flying or moving as a winged creature. Thus, it may easily be caught by the sticky glue on the kite's back when swooping lower in the dark. Toat wanted Cung would come on that special night. He asked if Cung did want to harvest a star. Cung shook his head, slowly said that he wasn't allowed to leave the home late at night, and promised not to tell anyone about Toat's will. It sounded better. He wanted to keep his own secret to avoid other people.

The last three nights of April, everything was prepared. Toat hid kite, string, and glue container under the roof of buffalo barn. Waking up at midnight, Toat silently handled kite, string, and glue and sneaked out of the house. He walked on an empty village road with strange emotions. When approaching the hills, Toat saw someone flying a kite. In the next field, two other men were pulling the string and went straight to the sky. Feeling uneasy, he went back home.

The next evening Toat's mother suddenly got a fever. He had to stay home to care for the sick. Though he's so sorry, but learning he could do nothing else. Sometimes he walked out to the front yard and looked up to thousands of stars sparkling like bunches of ripe fruit on the tree. With serious mind, Toat sent his wishes to a twinkling blue light star that his mother would get well soon.

The next day, Toat's mother got better and went to the fields. That led the buffalo herd to the foothill next to the river. He watched the large round rock on the top and felt regretful about past chance. He guessed, perhaps thousands of stars were traveling by this hill last night. They had left no traces except the blue sky bathed in the morning sunlight. Toat sadly thought he would have to wait until next year. He intended if Cung asked, Toat would tell the truth that his mother was sick last night, so he couldn't fly the kit. So Cung is not to label him as a liar.

In the middle of the quiet night, there was a small dramatic sound at the end of the bed. Toat sat up and saw his mother sleeping soundly. He intended to lie down and sleep again. But the quiet night outside made him think there may still be some stars once wandering across the river and stopping on the hilltop before flying into distant space. Toat gently got out of bed and went to the window to observe the night sky. Scattered here and there, some stars standing seriously as if on guard duty. A flash of pale light suddenly crossed the dark space. Perhaps a star moving closer to his village. Toat slowly opened the door and stepped out, tilted his head, and stared at a shadow of a white star floating on the Tinh Tu

River by the hill. Running to the barn where the kite and glue were hidden, Toat took them down and crept like a black cat down the dark village road.

There was no one to pick stars tonight, he knew it clearly. After brushing a thick glue layer on the kite, he climbed to the top of the rock and flew the kite higher into the air. His hands gently release the jute string. The kite caught wind swung under the dim light, then gradually moved upwards and disappeared into the dark. Unable to see anything in the vast space, Toat gently pulled the string back to probe the kite at the other end. But his fingers felt little resistance as he was holding a piece of wind. In the dark night, Toat passionately watched a star hanging on the top of the hill in a nervous mood. Above, there were thousands of stars crowded together in endless space. Then suddenly the sky's lit up with a million candle lights. A silver light flashed across the field, then flew toward the river and calmly disappeared. Toat stared intently at the string hanging high above and waiting. A few minutes later, countless tiny blue-white spots suddenly clinging on the string, making his fingers feel cooler. Guessing there must be something strange, Toat quickly took the kite back. When it went down lower, he was excited to see a bright blue-white spot sticking on it as a shining lamp.

When the kite landed on the hilltop, there was a star hanging loosely on its back. Toat was nervous as he watched the star five-tip occasionally flashing, shooting out tiny white particles that spread along the string. In the center of the star, there was a misty cloud that curled softly. When he touched it, Toat's fingers felt like they were dipping in a cold soft cotton bunch. A tingling feeling began to run through his both arms. In front of Toat, the five-wing star seemed to be cast from a block of clear and pure crystal mixed with white marble lying on the grass. Toat wanted to take it home and put it in a box. But the incredible joy of owning such a rare thing made Toat's little head dizzy. He tried to remember, then counted dreams on his fingers, and then gently touched the heart of the star as willing to put them all there. A blue light flashed along Toat's arm towards the heart beating in his chest. The star on the back of the kite began to fly up gently like a balloon, hovering in front of him to say goodbye.

Toat smiled as he looked at the star moving close to his face and then to the top of his head, randomly making hairs erecting upwards. The small clicking sounds were continuously bursting out. Toat's hair by the forehead got many tiny bright dots as if they were going to turn white. Finally, Toat looked up into space, both hands holding the string to fly the kite and the star on the wind to the sky. Fresh breezes blew the kite gradually higher into the dark. Toat stood still on the hilltop and moved up his neck to see the small white spot flying away. His blue star shone brightly and then joined the other stars floating within the glowing galaxy. Toat retrieved the kite and brought the container home. Lying on the bed, he curled up, hiding his hands under the blanket. But he felt likely a cool icy layer was clinging to his whole fingers. Toat smiled himself and closed his eyes.

The next afternoon, Cung appeared while Toat was watching a buffalo herd on the hillside. He asked Toat what he did last night. That said, at midnight he had been on the hilltop to fly a kite and finally harvest a star. Swiftly cutting across Toat's story, Cung said, he had known that Toat had picked a star already. Last night he couldn't sleep so he went to the upstairs window and looked towards the hill. Cung said seeing a star getting lower and lower. He didn't want to hide his story so he nodded. Cung asked, where was that star now? Toat pointed a finger to the sky. Cung's eyes so regretfully looking to the late noon sunlight shone above the blue clouds. Cung continuously questioned him, why let this star free? That explained, why he just wanted to look at twinkling stars in the sky every night. That it's. Over there, stars were freely floating over endless space. Cung looked at him with distrust. Toat showed out his hands and said his fingers had touched the star. At this time, both of them still were really cool. Cung held ten fingers for a few seconds and nodded with extreme surprise. Then he dropped Toat's fingers and said they were too cold. Next, Cung's soft black hair suddenly rose up, then emitting strange, small rattling sounds./.

TAN'S LITTLE SNAKE

Tan's family lives alone in a remote field. Their house was built between a green lush grove yard. On the east, his grandfather's home sat by the road running through the village. Every day, Tan and his brother walked to school on this shady road. Far to the left, there was a local force post had been built near a steel bridge that crossed a canal linked to the confluence. His father was a soldier of this post.

It's Saturday, his father got permission from his officer for a day off. He's back home to dredge the creek in the hind yard. This creek was dug by villagers a long time ago for irrigating rice fields.

oOo

It's midsummer over the Mekong Delta. The evening was coming but the sun in the west still shining over dry empty fields. Tan's father wore an old soldier khaki shirt and short drawers, a green khaki hat, held a hoe then stepped down the canal to clear nenuphar, water morning glory, grass, and weeds. He picked all of these plants and piled them in a corner. Then after, he dredged the bottom and brought silt, and mud and dumped them on the bank. Tan and his young brother came to help. They used buckets to dredge rotten plants, grasses, and weeds sinking deep in the muddy silt. Tan worked and then played at the same time. He handed a bamboo basket and tried to catch small fish, creatures that swim in the water. Toi, his brother just 12 or 13 years old but less talkative and more laborious. He didn't join with Tan. In this season, the water was low but clear and full of small fishes were swimming everywhere.

The sun's getting lower in the field. After fulfilling long dredging work, his father took a break on the bank, smoked, and watched Tan's brothers. He then ordered:

-Come and bring these branches to the bank, please
Lurking a gourami fish hid under a bunch of weeds, and heard his father's request, Tan and his brother said:
-Yes, dad

These rotten branches got here and tangled in the weeds, grass, nenuphars ... that blocked the stream in the canal. Toi stepped onto the bank, used his hands to tow branches stuck by wet and long weeds out of the water then put them in dry land. Every year, his father had to dredge once or twice to get clean water for home needs. Almost in the evening, Tan and his brother and sister came here to swim and play.

His father walked to faraway fields behind the post, where the water from the canal flowed into the canal. Only them here, Toi hardly dredged muddy soil with a bucket then poured them around tree trunk. Meanwhile, Tan eagerly caught fish in a bamboo basket. After got a small one under the grass, he called Toi:
-I got a gourami fish
-Let me see

Toi moved his finger to discard grasses, and weeds and watched a small fish then smiled:

-It's not gourami, it's betel fish

-We'll keep it

-No, there are a lot of gourami, and betel fish in the creek. Feeding lia thia, siam fish for fighting are funnier

Tan looked to his brother and then replied:

-Mom didn't like us feeding fighting fish and forgetting school lessons. Dad will give us some rod

Toi smiled:

-Don't let mom know this

From the source of the canal, his dad came back then watched the creek bed and said:

-Here's good. Move forward to clean the waterway behind our home before the break

Tan's brothers stepped into the bank. They walked to mature trees lined along the border of the orchard. There's a dead log crossing the creek as a bridge. Stood in it, Tan moved fast as an otter, he swiftly plunged into the middle of weeds, grasses, and nenuphar floating on the water. Toi also jumped from the bridge while holding the bucket. His father smiled and said:

-Tan, Toi ... let's pick up some nenuphar, lotus flowers for food. Do it quickly, before I dredge them all and throwing to the bank

Tan replied:

-Yes, Toi brings the basket over here

The country boys like them were experienced with swimming, dredging, catching fish, pick up wild vegetables. So, these works were really simple. They grasped nenuphar rods under water then brook it and rolled up. After a while, they filled up the basket with a lot of these wild plants. His father went down into the water and began dredging from a distance, then gradually moved back to the hind yard. When seeing fresh nenuphars, and lotus rods in the basket, he cheered:

-Good boys. Tan brings them all to your mom

-Yes, dad

Tan held the basket in the waist and ran under the orchard's canopies to the kitchen. He put all of them on the bamboo shelf and then went back outside. Under the fading sky in the west, they quickly picked up branches, dead leaves, and grasses … in the canal then dumped on the banks.

Evening's falling, tide from confluent pushed high water in the creek into smaller waterways stretched to far meadows. From remoted bushes, the sound of pied birds resounded harmoniously into the calm summer air. His father threw other bunches of nenuphar leaves among a pile of grasses and weeds. Tan sat nearby and saw some small snakes were extruding heads outside then crawling quickly into the water.

-There are some small snakes here – Tan pointed his finger to the leaves

Toi looked up and asked:

-Nenuphar snake?

-Right

Tan asked:

-Is it a venomous snake?

-Oh no, it's benign and unvenomous

While Tan stayed motionless, three then four tiny snakes fled and hid under grasses or slid to the creek. Curiously, he lifted some round nenuphar leaves to check anyone that still hid beneath. Some small shrimps were jumping wildly near black snails that lay motionless as dead. Beneath another leaf, Tan suddenly found a tiny snake moving its head with black, round eyes with fear. He stayed motionless for a while. Then touching the body of the tiny snake. But the little creature didn't want to move away.

-Yet another one, Tan?

-Yeap

The brother bravely touched the snake's head which made it raise its body into the air. Toi's overjoyed and did the same thing. The tiny snake proved its patience by swinging its small head. Said Tan:

-It's so gentle, not seeking for a hide

Toi asked his brother:

-Release it now?

-Yeap

Toi removed weeds bounded in its tail then gently making a touch as promote. But the snake made a little move and then stayed motionless. His brother stared and found out something new:

-Perhaps its tail had been disabled

Asked Toi:

-Is it true brother ... where?

His brother pointed a stick to the curved tail:

-Oh, yeap! The last part of its tail isn't good and strong so it hardly moves on

Toi said:

-Let it go free in the creek

Tan slowly put the tiny snake in the waterway. It moved the tiny body in several seconds then swam to the grasses and raised its head. He said in a low voice:

-It didn't want to swim away as others

Tan spoke then gently held the tiny snake to the old place. Toi felt sympathy and then said:

-Will we keep and feed it?

Tan agreed:

-Go home and bring the metal bucket that Dad carry back from the post

Toi quickly jumped up and ran on the log bridge then disappeared in the hind orchard. A moment later, he brought a small gray rectangle ammo container painting an army sign to the creek. He got some water into it. His elder brother added some more weeds. Then they put the tiny snake inside. There's a voice sounded through the orchard. Their youngest sister, named Nga appeared. She crossed the log bridge, got closed, and asked:

-What's inside?

Her two brothers moved heads back, and Tan replied:

-A tiny nenuphar snake

Nga sat next to Tan. She stared inside the box:

-Let me see it ... Does it bite?

-Dad said it's unvenomous and gentle. We'll take it home later

The youngest sister squinted at both brothers:

-What will we feed it?

Tan replied:

-Nenuphar snakes eat small fishes, and shrimp ... Each day we catch them here and then bring them home

Toi asked:

-How about Earth Worm brother? There are a lot in the orchard

His big brother may be facing a hard question. He thought for some moments and then replied in a low tone:

-Yeah, maybe it can

His father got nearer and watched the box through three small children's heads:

-What's inside ... Lia thia fishes?

Tan replied:

-No dad, nenuphar snake

-It's late evening. All of you take a bath then go home. I'm home first for dinner. Tonight, I have to guard the post.

The sun was just an orange ball on the horizon. Tide was rising up to the tree lines on the bank. Tan's brothers and sister were swimming and playing in the clean waterway run through the tranquil field until their mom called them back for dinner.

oOo

From the day they caught the tiny snake, Tan was the most laborious among his brothers. In the morning, they walked to school. Afternoon, he carried a bamboo basket and then caught small fish in the creek to feed the snake. Sometimes Tan found small worms in the orchard instead of fish. He's happy when the small snake loves ground worms either.

When the water in the box got murky, Tan asked his brother to change it to a clean one. Likely the tiny nenuphar snake loved to live in a metal box, so it didn't try to escape. For the first time, when their mother had seen the metal box on the bamboo shelf, she asked them some questions and then forgot. Their father went forth and back between the post and home, so he's not interested. Tan's brother and sister after school time had much time to play either with their friends or the snake.

In the evening, before going to bed, Tan put the lid loosely on the box, so the tiny snake had enough fresh air to breathe. Then he put it back on the shelf.

Sometime in the night, the gun sound echoed back from across the river or remote fields behind their home. These horrible sounds often scare children in the country like Tan's brothers and sisters.

Tan's brothers carefully fed and took care of the tiny snake so it grew up quickly. After a month, its size was nearly Tan's thumb. Now it can eat more fish, and worms and slither strongly inside the box.

In the evenings or holidays, Tan often induced Men or Tong, his school friends to visit his home and see their snake. Men used their fat fingers to touch the snake's head and then burst into laughter. Tong watched a while then turned his head toward Tan and said:
-We go to the creek behind home and catch some fish to feed it
Men eagerly said:

-Yeah. Go now

Put the bucket on the shelf, Tan led his two friends to a kitchen wing. They took a bamboo basket and a tin can and then rushed through the orchard to the log bridge. Tong held a basket and then jumped to the creek. He walked along the grass to catch small fish. After got some, he poured them into the can. Men took the basket from Tong's hands and then moved to deeper waterway. He caught some more betel fishes. Tan looked inside the can and then said:

-That's enough. Now we swim

Three boys largely jumped from the bridge into the creek and threw flash water away. They swam and joked so noisy under the blueish and shining hot sky. A moment later, Toi appeared under the tree line. He quickly undressed and joined the bridge jump game with Tan and two neighbors. Their joking noise resounded to a whole corner of the rice field.

The sun was setting down slowly in the west. His mother had come back from his grandparent home, she carried the bucket to the creek and called:

-Toi brings me a bucket of water to cook a meal

-Yes mom

The young brother carried a bucket to the bank then scooped clean water in the creek and brought it back home. Tan and Men quickly brought two more buckets home and then kept the game ahead. Finally, they left the creek and brought fish back home to feed the snake. Tong induced them:

-Another day, Tan ... you carry the snake into class to show it to others

He smiled:

-Yes, next weekend I will bring it to the class. Both of you don't tell to anyone before.

Men likely loved the Nenuphar snake. So before leaving, he carried it to the small couch and caressed it like a kitty cat. Fed with a lot of fish, the snake slithered to all corners as it wanted to play with three boys that overjoyed and smiled with half eyes closed.

The next Friday, Tan picked two round nenuphar leaves in the creek and then secretly put them together with the tiny snake inside his school bag.

At school, in a corner of the play yard, his two friends, Men and Tong waited for him under the shade of a tamarind tree. They calmly asked:
-Hey Tan, did you bring the snake along with you?
-Yes, I will show it when class breaks for playtime

Class time began with the loud sounds of drums. Tan and his two best friends were the last to queue. First hours in the morning, Miss Hai, a woman teacher, taught them a short spelling lesson. Then after, there was a writing lesson as usual. She wrote sentences with chalk on the blackboard. The whole students quietly wrote to the white papers with full care. Tan's sitting between Men and Tong at the last table of the class. The trio now and then smiled together causing Hoa, another boy to sit alone near them paying attention. Writing some words, Men moved his hand to touch Tan's school bag. It's about breaking time. From the rear side, Hoa stretched his body towards Tan, and quietly said:

-Hey, a tiny snake in your school bag

Tan has turned back then making a sign to calm him. The snake was suffocated and slithered outside, raising its head and looking around. Hoa dropped his pen, pulled the bag then cried:

-It's crawling outside

Tan pushed his hand away. The snake dropped onto the floor. The noise-induced other pupils to sit around them. They looked down and saw the snake near Tan's foot. Someone yelled:

-Snake ... snake

Ms. Hai turned back from the blackboard:

-Quiet! Let's write the homework

A dozen mouths screamed:

-Snake in the class, teacher

Ms. Hai's showed a big surprise. Her eyes widened and looked down. Loud cries of a broken bee hive scared the tiny snake. It's slithering around the classroom floor. Tan, Men, and Tong stooped down to catch it under the wooden banks. Over a dozen female pupils sitting in opposite rows climbed onto tables, banks then screamed. Their teacher now feared and stayed motionless in the stand. Hoa spoke loudly to the boy pupils:

-Hey friends, nenuphar is not venomous, not bite

The boys jumped down from the banks. All of them now tried to catch the tiny snake and burst into funny laughter as in a feast. But the tiny snake quickly dodged their hands. It quickly slithered to the door and rushed to the grasses in the drainage. Timely the drum sounded twice to alert the break moment. All of the class ran to the yard like a small wave. Ms. Hai had known Tan brought a snake into class. So she asked:

-Tan, why did you go to school with a snake?

Afraid to be punished, he then tells a lie:

-Yes ... It moved to my school bag in the evening, so I didn't see

Just after his teacher's quest, Tan was allowed to get out of the class. Men, Tong, and Hoa are standing and waiting for him nearby. They walked close:

-We have to seek the snake, Tan

They walked to the other side of the class then searched along the drainage to the barbed wire fence and stopped there. The snake disappeared among thick bushes and plants growing towards the creek. Hoa was squinting his eyes and said:

-Perhaps it runs to over there

In his thoughts, Tan's worried and regretted either. Ms. Hai's husband is also a soldier at a local post. Sometimes he together with two, or three other soldiers visited Tan's home. They brought along some fish, shrimp, and crabs to cook food then drank wine with his father. This was a young and funny soldier. Private Duc had tanned skin, was quite handsome, and often smiled with every person. Tan regretted the runaway snake that he and his brother had loved and fed for a long time.

That afternoon, he went back to school alone to seek the snake. But seeing Mr. Truong, a supervisor was standing in the corridor in front of his classroom, so he had to walk out. Next Saturday, all the teachers and pupils were off. Tan got back to school again. He walked around the drainage for a while before seeing his tiny snake hiding in the grasses. Tan recognized the curved tail and carried it home with big joy.

At last, his father knew the whole story in the classroom. Duc, Ms. Hai's husband told the pupils in Tan's class that he had dropped the lesson, in pursuit of his snake.

After his military operation had ended on the other side of the river, Tan's father brought home some canned foods and a parcel of sugar. He ordered the Tans brothers to release the snake. He worried that Tan's brothers couldn't study well.

Tan and his brother brought the metal box to the tree line on the bank and then released their nenuphar snake. The tiny creature likely didn't want to flee away. It swam around lotus and nenuphar flowers next to the bank. Sometimes it raised a small head towards Tan then dived into grasses and reappeared in the same place. Said Toi:

-Now back home

Several days later, when Toi's learning school lessons in the evening, he heard some noise rustling on the floor then slightly touching his foot. Bend down and saw a snake, he lifted both feet up and then screamed:

-Brother, snake's slithering into home

-Where ... where?

Toi handled the army torch shone it down then said:

-Nenuphar snake

-Really?

Tan stepped closer. He caught it and then put it on the table. His sister, Nga stood next to him and smiled:

-It's very smart, still knew the way back to our home

The trio sitting around and watching the tiny snake as a pet dog. Tan's happy when it didn't move away and stayed in the creek behind the orchard.

For almost several days, the tiny snake slithered to Tan's feet while he learning school lessons in the evening. And when every person went to bed, it quietly slithered back to the creek. There were a lot of small fishes living in the grasses, weeds, and nenuphars ... So it got a lot of food to eat and grew bigger.

When Tan brothers swam in the creek, the snake often appeared and swam around them. But not move far away from the place where Tan had seen it before. Men, Tong walked to their home to watch the snake. They loved to sit under the natural trees looking it swam around. Then all of them took off dresses and swam until evening came down.

oOo

The dry season has passed when the rains from the seashore fall over rice fields in the delta. On a long rainy night bursting with frogs, and toads sound in the dark, the post was attacked by some mortars from guerillas hiding across the river. Heavy explosions have awakened and terrified people. Two missing mortars hit the creek then exploding as thunder behind Tan's home. The whole family had to rush to the underground cover beneath the wooden couch until the quiet air turned back.

In the morning, Tan walked towards the orchard. He saw fallen branches and leaves scattering in the ground. The creek has been hit by a mortar. Here, he couldn't see any green grasses, weeds, nenuphars, and lotus floating in the water as so far. All of them were scattered into every corner of the fields. That day, Tan's sad all the time. He thought the tiny snake got the same fate together with other wild plants.

The next afternoons, each time he got there, Tan's walking along the creek to seek his nenuphar snake. But just small fishes swam in from the river.
One day, he sat and thought a while then brought back nenuphar, lotus, and weeds from another place and grew them in the creek with little hope.

Half a month later, the things that he brought back now quickly grew up green and floating in the water.

When there was no rain in the afternoon, Tan sat under the natural tree line and watched the clean waterways and rice fields rattling in the wind.

On a rare beautiful afternoon with bright sunlight shining after a fresh shower, Tan's done school lessons and sat on the log bridge to wait. Round nenuphars' leaves still held tiny water drops that twinkled like silver beads. He saw the tiny snake raising its head from a bunch of weeds and swam gently. Tan was overjoyed and greeted it as a dear friend just come back from a long trip./.

THE DEADLY BLOW

In 1942, world war broke out across the Eurasian and African continents, then slowly spreading to Indochina countries. Mr. Lam and his brother, who owned shops in Hanoi, began to feel uneasy. He quickly went to his brother's house to discuss the idea that temporarily turning back to their hometown in the country. The two brothers sat at the table in the middle room and drank tea. The brother asked:

-Was your tea shop in good business?

Mr. Lam replied:

-Not so good. Everyone now is afraid of war and famine, so they spend less. Did your products sell well?

The older brother thoughtfully shook his head:

-Me too, only a few old customers came

-I plan to take a break for a while and bring my family back to Bac Giang province. When the war ended, we will return to Hanoi for business again

-Why do you look so worried?

Mr. Lam replied:

-The situation in Hanoi seems not good. It was worsened. Business time by time going down. Tea traders from the highlands bring less and less goods down here

-Did they say anything else?

-Nothing. But as you know, is there any news?

The brother nodded:

-I have heard some people who trade traditional medicine from provinces near the Chinese border to Hanoi, saying they sometimes meet groups of people against the French, and even the Japanese in the mountains

Mr. Lam immediately asked:

-Are they Viet Minh?

-Probably, people I knew in Hanoi also say the same

-What did they say about these groups?

The brother said:

-Some Hanoi people seemingly were afraid ... It is rumored that the Viet Minh operating secretly in all major cities

He sighed:

-I'm afraid that if the Allies attack the Japanese army here, we won't be able to escape in time

The elder brother thought silently for a moment then said:

-Yes... it would be good if you and your family returned there for a while. Who knows, if there's fighting here, I have to take my wife and children back to the country with your

-I'll beg your care to my home and goods here. My eldest son will also stay in Hanoi

The brother smiled:

-Yes, I will daily send my assistant come over to help him to do business. When you are back in Bac Giang, please find more sources of goods and send them here to me. So when would you go?

-Thank you very much. The plan is the day after tomorrow

The brother advised:

-Yes, when you are in the hometown, and meet Mr. Hoi, my old friend living in a nearby village, please send my regards

After greeting his brother, he walked out into the street. Mr. Lam's heart was full of anxious thoughts. Hanoi streets were empty in the late afternoon. Herbal medicine shops on the street were quite calm with some opening for business. A light fragrance wafted in the hot, dry summer air.

They were born in Bac Giang province, in the northeast of Hanoi. Lived there until he was nearly fifteen years old, the father brought the family to Hanoi under the guidance of their uncle, who had a tea shop near Hang Phen Street. This year, he was nearly fifty years old. He's very familiar with the streets, lakes, and houses in this charming city. On the road, some military vehicles carrying French soldiers silently watch the passengers on the streets while their vehicles move towards Long Bien bridge.

On the European continent, German tanks rolled through Paris and occupied almost all of France's territory.

oOo

Returned to his family's old house in a village next to a small river flowing lazily through the fields, Mr. Lam began repairing damage in the roof and began growing vegetables and trees in the garden with the help of his cousin next door. The first busy week, he visited friends in the village. With the thought of a business people, seeing almost all young boys and men were free after working in the fields which waste time and could breed bad things. He borrowed the temple yard and then started a free martial arts class to train them about physical strength and mental mind.

The first evening class only had three young men near his house. The teacher and students practiced enthusiastically under trees' shadows. He recalled the martial moves that he had learned from his uncle. The young uncle once living in Hoi An near Da Nang had learned from a Japanese martial arts master. Being a Hanoi man with a sophisticated mind, he modified and simplified the close combat arts with weapons into easy-to-understand lessons. The villagers gradually respected and loved their long-time neighbor who returned from Hanoi. They asked him to open other classes for poor illiterate children. Though the wartime was difficult, they often gave him some fruits and vegetables … grew in the gardens. This goodwill made him love the old village even more.

Gradually, the reputation of his martial arts class spread to nearby villages. So more young people came to learn. The number now has reached fourteen people. He observed each student's physical character and temper before teaching different martial arts exercises. A few months later, he found two young men around sixteen and seventeen who were clever and quick learners. Both of them, were boys have agile and strong appearances of good martial fighters. The first, named Tu living in his village, was gentle, honest, and humble. The other, living a nearby village on a northern hill hamlet. He was a bit short but vigorous and quiet. His name was Hoach, son of a buffalo trader in the highland. His family was well-off, and his father wished his son got some martial arts to defend himself.

Every weekend, Mr Lam planned for two senior students to compete with each other in the temple yard. Most villagers came to see their sons. Usually, every fighting match between Tu and Hoach was good, and everyone praised them. Tu has a gentle offensive but hides immense strength inside. Hoach often unleashes powerful and agile moves like a fierce hurricane. The two were equal and qualified boxers. After a long time watching these two students in the dual fight, he noticed when Hoach won, he still kept a normal demeanor and happily chatted with his opponent. On the contrary, Hoach behaved angry and ashamed when he was defeated and quickly left.

These things made him think so much about teaching other martial arts moves, including sophisticated, deadly closed combat ways. Especially when it was used by bad people who want to rob and kill others.

Living in a small town was quite easier than a big city. He often went to the hilly villages to see some tea merchants to buy their goods and then send them to Hanoi. But business became increasingly difficult as war spread from remote mountains to the delta.

oOo

Time has passed quickly. Mr. Lam has been here for nearly two years.

This Sunday he went to see an old friend. Since returning to Bac Giang till now, he used to visit Mr. Hoi in a nearby village.

Meeting each other, they talked about new and old stories. Mostly they were concerned about the war now raging from the Pacific islands to the far border of India, and the French colonial moves while the Japanese army seized Indochina. Seeing him walking through the gate, Mr. Hoi was watering the flower pots, then ceased and said:

-Good morning, have some tea with me

-Thank you. How are you? Are you still teaching to earn a living?

Mr. Hoi smiled, then walked to the round table under the veranda, poured hot tea into two cups, and replied:

-Yes... Let's have some tea. Any news? Is your brother's business in Hanoi good?

- Still the same, whenever possible

They sat on chairs next to the wooden table, looking at the flowers blossoming in the garden. The summer sunlight in the east shone brightly on the high canopies. After enjoying a few tea cups, Mr. Hoi said:

-The morning sun is nice, we have to take a walk along the river to cool down. The air out there is fresh now

He nodded:

-Yes, that's good

The homeowner went inside to change clothes. Then they walked out of the gate, strolling along the deserted road and thatched houses towards the riverbank. They climbed up the low dike and slowly walked farther upstream. Finding a calm place, there was a green corn field stretching to the horizon, they sat under a large tree shade overlooking the clear water of the river. Mr. Lam looked around and said:

-Today we went further than before

-Yes, this place has beautiful scenery

Mr. Hoi smiled and watching the dim silhouette of hills and mountains emerging at the end of the fields across the river asked:

-What do farmers in your village grow in this season?

-When it's dry, they grow sweet potatoes, and so does my family

-Peasants are often poor, and war is even more miserable. Over here is the French, and in the south is the Japanese. Now France is likely losing the war. The Japanese army probably won't be humble for longer

-If Japan ousts France in Indochina, would the allies attack?

-That's right, allied planes will bomb where Japanese soldiers are stationed. Have you heard anyone in your village talking about the Viet Minh?

Mr. Lam replied:

-Some people came back from Cao Bang and Lang Son talking about them. Have you heard this before?

Mr. Hoi pointed his hand to the distance in the northwest hills across the river:

-Yes, here they have told me, that Viet Minh had been active in those areas for a long time. Many villages in the upstream and across this river now also see their men. They operate very secretly

-When I was in Hanoi, some people said they were friends of the allies

-Yes, the Viet Minh were very clever. They won the support of Mao's army. Now both sides are still fighting across Europe and Asia, they're waiting patiently for an opportunity to overthrow the French

-I think so. A professor in Hanoi said their ideology came from Russia and goes against Western countries

-I think that's a worry matter. They are relying on China for hideouts and weapons. Support the workers, farmers classes ...

On the tranquil space, some boats go up and down the upper and lower stream. Two shepherds wearing conical hats lead their buffaloes down to cool off in the blue water. The countryside scenery is so quiet under the hot sunlight.

oOo

Though leaving Hanoi, Mr. Lam and his family live in Bac Giang was often linked with news from every corner of Indochina. A few times he returned to Hanoi for some business and learning the war news, then quickly moved back to his hometown. Over time the martial arts class in the village had fewer and fewer students. The two best students, Tu and Hoach, were still present. He taught both of them advanced moves to be used in close combat, making everyone feel enthusiastic. But Hoach's temper was getting worse and worse. During a dual fight, Hoach who was stronger so overwhelmed Tu, but the village boy always avoided all his rival's fierce attacks. At last, Tu quickly swiped his foot and threw Hoach to the ground. Hoach felt shame like an underdog then jumped up with anger. While everyone didn't pay attention after fighting time ended, Hoach punched Tu hard in the back for revenge and quickly left.

From then on, Mr. Lam did not teach more keen moves to this aggressive student. On the other hand, separately, he instructed Tu to the higher skills to fight back armed people. But Hoach is a very skeptical person. After class time was over, he pretended to walk away but secretly sneaked back to watch. The goodwill of a Hanoi man couldn't change the bad mind of a youngster. But Hoach had resented the martial arts master so much.

One day, after practicing some fighting with Mr Lam, Hoach suddenly started to quarrel with a younger student who incidentally collided with him. He rushed to attack but was stopped by Tu and others. With angry words, he cursed, stared at Tu, and shouted:

-Don't jump in my business, because you have learned more than me. One day you will pay the price

Hoach arrogantly left the class. Since then, Mr. Lam has not seen him return to martial arts class again.

Quite a long time passed, and a young man in the village met Mr Lam in the temple yard and told him a story about Hoach. His student had left home on the hill. He went to the northern highland with a clang of buffalo traders. Prominent in martial arts skills, he was highly respected. That fresh news startled him. But thinking Hoach was only using it for self-defense, he wasn't too worried.

oOo

The hot summertime in the highlands just passed. The mild weather in early fall was quite cool. Saturday morning Mr. Lam made a stroll outside the village and then visited Mr. Hoi.

They sat under the veranda with a teapot on the round table, talking about war news until the sun rose higher in the blue sky. Mr. Lam stood up to say goodbye and left.

The sun shone over the calm air. He opened the umbrella and leisurely walked along the dike foot to the edge of the village. As he stepped between two rows of thick thorny bamboo trees, Mr. Lam folded the black umbrella to avoid the bamboo branches and slowly walked over the dead leaves on the ground. His ears listened to the whispering wind from the river blowing through the tree lines. His mind thinking about new events in neighboring countries. The Indochina peninsular situation quickly changed when World War II ended a month ago. Ally armies had won the war in Europe and the Asia Pacific. There are rumors that French colonists would move back to Indochina countries in the coming month. Mr. Hoi this morning was pessimistic about the life of the Viet Nam people. The old teacher pointed to the north and said:

- Vietnam would be miserable if Chiang Kai-shek lost control of China's continent and retreated to the Pacific islands near the mainland seashore. Once, our fate is decided by another

Mr. Lam remembered his old friend's sad eyes while watching the peaceful countryside scene. He looking the white mince clouds wandering in early autumn trying to guess something would happen in the gray sky. His feet moved while his mind kept thinking about what Mr. Hoi had said about the guerrilla squads in the country. They just returned and operating across the river. Among them was a group led by a young man skilled in martial arts, who specialized in assassinating the French soldiers, and officials and collecting taxes. In his mind, he remembered the old student named Hoach. But in his thought, he was still doing the family business. While passing by between thick bamboo bushes growing along the narrow trail, suddenly a tall, young sturdy man steps out to block his way. After an amazed moment when the young man in black clothes smiled at him, Mr.

Lam recognized he was Hoach. Seeing the handle of the machete exposed under his old student's shirt lap on the left, he briefly thought of something bad. He asked:

-It's a long time since you have left the class. How is your family's business on the upper hill these days?

His cunning, sharp eyes flashed with hatred. But his mouth still smiling while greeting:

-Hello teacher, it's been a long time since we saw each other.

He paused for a few seconds and then continued:

-You just came back from your old friend in the neighboring village, right?

-Yes, I just visited an old friend there...

The country noon air in early autumn suddenly became harsh, dry, and quiet among the bamboo bushes. Hoach's eyes stared at him and said:

-He is a traitor who serves as a lackey for the French

Hearing this vague accusation, Mr. Lam calmly replied:

-He is a gentle teacher, not a lackey for anyone. On the other hand, he was a patriot and opposed the French army

Hoach stood still. He seemed confused and then turned to something else:

-When I was learning martial arts, you had a disdainful attitude towards me and behaved badly compared to other students. You secretly taught Tu the keen fighting arts while I was not there. You look down on my poverty

-I have taught in different ways up to each student's condition. To me, people deserve to be respected for their dignity, not rich or poor

The student smirked and quickly pulled out the sharp machete from his waist and said:

-Today I want to fight with you to see who will win

Mr. Lam knew Hoach had been waiting for a long time for this good opportunity to kill him. In this narrow space and without a weapon, it was difficult to compete with a strong, young man armed with a sharp blade. As a master, Mr Lam recalled this arrogant student was very impatient and eager to win, he showed out the wooden handle of the umbrella made of old hard bamboo and said:

-If your keen blade can cut off this handle, then I lose and you win

With a contemptuous smile, Hoach raised machete and slashed hard. It chopped down the bamboo handle so sweetly, and unexpectedly Hoach lost momentum and leaned to the left side. Mr. Lam, as quick as lightning, stabbed the sturdy sharp umbrella handle upward. It pierced the student's throat. Mr. Lam's hand spun the handle so hard. Hoach died with widened eyes.

The following week, Mr. Hoi visited him in a calm morning. They walked on shining village road and greeted some people. They viewed the beautiful countryside with green rice fields, buffalo herd grazing, and some young boys flying kites, some swimming in the river. Mr Hoi suddenly asked if he had heard that a guerrilla commander had been killed on the dike road between two villages. Mr. Lam calmly shook his head and said:

-I do not know anything./.

THE FUNERAL MAN MOURNS THE SEA

He has done this job for a long time. It was hereditary work that was inherited from his father. And his father had inherited from his grandfather. When his father passed, he succeeded in burying the dead. However, his grandfather and father weren't professional funeralmen. When there were no funerals in their poor village, they were laborious farmers on small fields at the foothills next to the Truong Son range that was often covered by foggy clouds.

In this village, only his family and a few other people were farmers. The real reason, they have no boat to sail and fish in the sea. The rest of the more than twenty others were all fishermen. It was a traditional job. Similar to his funeral work.

The central region land of Viet Nam is less fertile but so arid. People there have often undergone natural disasters. Every year, sea storms rushed inland, creating floods and tropical swirl winds swept along the shore. Eventually, the raging wind encountered the high mountains in the west, it swang back towards coastal villages and sat on the narrow plains. Those wild winds as crazy horses unleashed their hooves, galloping wildly throughout the low lands with unstoppable race. They destroyed fields, gardens, crops, homes ... and sometimes killed a lot of people.

The most terrifying thing happened when these winds mixed with flash floods from Truong Son mountains to sweep across slopes, took down large logs then crushed small villages in the lowlands, wreaking horrible disasters and dead.

At those times, he had to work all the time. Most of the day, he had stayed in the cemetery next to the white sandy hills lined by old poplar trees. Relentlessly, he dug graves to bury the dead.

Out of those disasters, the village by the cove has experienced a quiet life as it got a hundred years ago. According to some oldest people, men and young boys of this village were strong and brave fishermen. They're too familiar with fishermen's lives often daring by waves and deep sea. Naturally, the village was poor for decades. Most of them were illiterate. Some people didn't know how to write down their true fathers and mother's names. But in return, God gave them virtues of good seamen. Watched out water currents and clouds, they could predict fish-way and foreseen ocean hurricanes. Combined with distinct bravery, the villagers were famous as diligent men in this coastal region.

In the early mornings, under the misty air, overwhelmed by the wave sounds crashing to the beaches along old poplar wood, they sailed out to the open sea, where large fish were running and chasing bait that burst a large area. Over there, other fishermen's boats rarely dared to cast nets. For them, the sea was their second home, and waves were long-time friends.

In the late afternoon, after hours of sailing in the windy sea, their heavy boats were filled with shrimps and fish. They returned and moored to the pier, while women and children sheltering the hot sun under shades and waiting. They laughed, and calling voices from the crowds filled the beaches. The traders bargained for fresh fish and shrimp. Then cars drove them to big cities and towns sat dozens of kilometers away. Their fish and shrimp baskets would be sent to markets, restaurants, food stores ...

oOo

Daily life in his small village went as well as past generations. Sea donated good meals, and warm clothes to those gentle people. Sometimes, the sea had reversed its routine way, threw rogue winds, and crashed their boats and men into the depths forever. In those days, the villagers suffered from sadness and agonies.

Though his main career was funeral man, when someone found a temporary fisherman, he sailed with them either to share some fish or shrimps from the catch to ease his family life. In these times, he even felt the strong tie between villagers and the sea. Although this distrusted sea had buried their cousins, and friends under cruel waves. He usually thought that life in his village would go constantly so far. The next generations of descendants also sailing and fishing as a tradition and heritage.

So far, the vast sea was a giant treasure that gave them a good life through the years. Then suddenly one day, shocking news emerged. He and other villagers have heard about the province's plan to build a big industrial park along the coast, quite distant from his village. Someone said it would be located to the north, in a deep and wide bay. So, ships with huge loads could easily sail in and out of the wharf after factories operate. But not only his village, dozens of fishing villages along the coast were worrying about it. They're poor, uneducated fishermen who spent all year around within boats, sea, and fish. Didn't know about steel or metallurgy ... That business was beyond their understanding. What they were interested in the most, their province would have a modern industrial park, then huge factories would spring up, providing jobs for people from rural villages. Since then, the country has stepped up to an industrialization and prosperity era.

In his heart, it was happiness mixing with worries. Perhaps all villagers as old as him got this same feeling. They thought their life on a fishing boat so far couldn't make the whole village get rich. They only could feed their families. Now, there would be modern factories, the whole village hoped better jobs could change their lives. But everyone was quite worried. It was new to their lives.

All of them just discussed it. Then everyone had to sail out to the sea to feed their families. Meanwhile, far away to the north, industrial parks and factories have been built day and night. Morning or evening, every time he went to the beach, he and some villagers stood under the poplar wood to watch that far side. They only saw a misty sky or some rumbling sounds filling the calm space. It was like they were blasting the bedrocks with dynamite. Then calmness came back again. At night, a huge bright light illuminated the far sea bay. They were listening while pushing the boats against the waves then went to sea. In the morning, when returning to the pier, their boats were still filled with fish and shrimp.

oOo

A few years passed, and his life and the other villagers continued with old traditions. There were dead people. He buried them in the cemetery and rest in peace. There were newborn children. They grew up and running, jumping, and playing on the village's winding road towards the beach. Here, people often listened to bargain voices and saw vehicles and boats carrying bamboo baskets full of sea products.

Several months passed, and he heard new factories would start to operate. In his village, some young men enthusiastically packed their bags and applied for some work there. Undoubtedly, they left their homes, and quit their traditional job as fishermen.

Sometimes, when having free time, he stood under the wood shade, squinting to the faraway side. But like other villagers, he couldn't see the real picture of a factory as wishing. The industrial park was quite out of their sight.

Only in clear daylight, he could watch two or three tall chimneys rising into the air like rice stalks. Some people from the neighboring village quit their work and make a trip to see it. When turned back, they said the park was a giant one.

Early December was coming. The northeast wind has blown over his village from the high mountains and poplar wood. As a routine, in the morning, some fishermen got up earlier. They walked to the beach, then started a sailing day out to sea to fish. In the dim darkness and gentle waves rustling on the sand, they saw dead fishes, large and small, were thrown onto the shore, scattered in small piles. Some of them couldn't believe in their eyes. They stepped close and picked up the big fishes that once swam agilely in the ocean, now lay dead. Horrible fear appeared on their face. People kept walking along the bay shore watching dead fishes begin changing their colors. Meanwhile, ocean waves constantly push more motionless fish to the shore.

Bad news from the beach spreading into the inland houses. The whole village seemed to be grilled on a big fire. Everyone quickly ran towards the sea. He followed the old fisherman next door. They were standing under the poplar wood shade. Before his eyes was a frightening scene that he had never seen since the day he was born until now. Dead fishes were gathering into large and small piles scattering along the waterside.

From the open sea, waves constantly brought dead ocean creatures to shore. There were so many dead fish that people didn't want to clean up or collect them in the first hours. The sun slowly shone, and the bright yellow sand color almost changed to dull gray-white. That's the color of death and destructive nature.

The tragic scene covered almost every fishing village along the coast, not just his. The news spread to every corner. People were confused. After weeks, they asked each other why the fish's death lasted for nearly half a month. Life got darkened. A lot of speculation from people and every corner...

Anyway, the villagers have to sail out to make a living. But the calamity lurking in the depths. The seabed now was almost empty. Their boats turned back with empty baskets, or with a bunch of small fishes. No town traders came to deal. The rumors of contaminated sea water spreading everywhere. At last, they didn't even dare to eat those fish.

Suspicious eyes began turning toward the silent factories. Looming chimneys still constantly billowing thick smoke into the sky. From underground running to the sea bed, some strange things happened that no one could see.

He sat there, watching the boats sleeping on the sand. Under the cool shade of the wood, there was no business in the afternoon. He recalled the images of people bursting into laughter, the bargaining sound, the roars of traffic ... He loved to watch boats full of fish sailing back from the sea. To him, it seemed the sea was dead. No more creatures swimming in it. His old eyes gazed at the quiet scenery around him. Somebody watched thoughtfully out to the open sea. Near the water's edge, a few small dead fishes with their soulless eyes and exhausted bodies were thrown up by the waves and lay there. He has seen the dull image of his village. It was overwhelming with grieves and sadness.

The old man felt hopeless. Tears from his fainted eyes silently went down to the sand. When some villagers passed away, he buried them in the small cemetery next to Poplar Wood. But when the sea died, he had nowhere to bury. Just the sea was too big./.

THE GREEN MEADOW AND SUNNY SUMMER

The bright sunlight filled the large meadow stretching to the faraway tree line next to the southern village. Summer season just came to the suburb of Saigon city. The west wind created twisting hot air in the still space, inventing tiny sounds howling over quiet vegetable gardens.

Tham, a girl from a nearby village, resting on a bucket by the water pump. She's just cleared some weeds and watered some radish, lettuce beds in her family garden. Sun was faded in the calm horizon. The neighbours next to her house now leaving their garden.

The deadly pandemic still terrifies people everywhere even her village. This large meadow was far from nearby villages, so Tham needn't mask her face when staying alone. Perhaps the sun and wind here have cleaned the air that flowing on the fields. Now the sun's going down in the west. She held her hat and intended to walk back home. From nowhere in the far green tree line, a young man appears under the faint light. On the other side of the meadow, Tham calmly watched the stranger wandering through swathes of vegetables. She thought seemingly he had gotten lost.

A moment later, the stranger saw Tham. He slowly walked on a small trail towards her. The young man's just 20 years old, without a mask, standing from a short distance then smiled and asked :
-Are you working in this garden?
Tham put his hand into his pocket to find a mask. She felt a little upset and hesitated to reply, then just nodded her head. Pointing his hand to the village hiding behind tree lines, he said :

- I'm living over there. Is your house nearby?

She nodded as the previous time. But her vigilant eyes didn't make the young man leave. He showed himself fun and did not hurry, then watched the quietness of vegetable gardens.

Tham watched his gentle, handsome face that sometimes glanced toward her and waited. The young man slightly moved his feet and looked down. She watched at his sandals and then said:

-You're standing near the ant nest

He smiled:

-Really, thank you

Trying to avoid the tiny angry ants, the young man stepped away and said:

-Can I sit here?

-Yes, you can

Sat right on the ground, he said:

-Do not worry, now I'm safe. It's cool and fresh here

She watched his T-shirt having blue and black stripes, then the brown khaki shorts that were like a Western guy. He said:

-I'm Tuong. What's your name?

-I'm Tham

-Do every day you bring vegetables to market?

Tham replied:

-No, the whole buyers will come

-Must you water the garden daily?

She pointed a finger to the water pump sitting under the plastic sheet near the well :

-Every day I have to water the vegetable beds to keep them fresh before picking up

On the large meadow, the sky sinks into darker air. The young man said:

The evening is about to come. I have to leave. Where is your home, Tham?

She turned her head to the faraway houses on the left:

-Yes, over there

-OK, bye. Good way home. You will be here every day?

Tham replied:

-Yes, when I must water or pick up vegetables

oOo

The next afternoon, Tuong got to the garden sooner. He met Tham's father just stopped the water pump. The engine sounds still echoing in the air. Standing in the distance, he said:

-Good afternoon

Mr Nuoi looking at Tuong and making a brief investigation. Tham pointed her hand to the far village behind the tree line:

-His name is Tuong, living over there. Yesterday Tuong had walked to this garden

Her father squinted at the tree lines:

-I knew, those new houses had been built just three years ago.

He replied:

-Right

-It's a long way when you walk from there

-Yes

He wore a hat and said to his daughter

-Tham, you need to clear more weeds then back home

Turn toward Tuong, he smiled:

-Bye, I will go home now

Now just Tuong and Tham stayed in the garden. He sat near the pump watching Tham clear weed between the vegetable beds and said:

-These vegetables look so good and fresh. When will the whole buyers come?

She moved up her head :

-Almost several days

-Uhu

Tham explained:

-These female buyers buy a lot of vegetables here and then deliver them to other retailers in the city markets

He pointed a finger to a small leave vegetable:

-What is the name of this vegetable?

-Coriander

-And over there?

-Celery

-Near your place is Amaranth, right?

-Yeap

Tuong smiled:

-Surely, you know the names of many vegetables?

-Of course, we farmers can recognize them all

-How many years has your family had this nice garden?
She smiles:
-Almost ten years. My dad was the main worker
Tham quietly cleared the weeds. Tuong looked at her and then moved his eyes to the surrounding gardens. After work was done, she cleaned her hands in the plastic bucket by the pump. Tuong sent another small bucket to her and sat on his yesterday place. She smiled and thought Tuong was so careful to keep an adequate distance.
-Tuong, where do you work now?
-I am a student, now studying in London, UK. Like here, Europe was raging by the pandemic, so I must go home. I've been in Saigon for about ten days. It's too boring to sit all day with a computer in my room. So, I tried to walk outside for fresh air
Tham looked at Tuong's appearance and asked:
-How long have you studied over there?
-I've studied computer science and almost completed the second year. All the homes in my area shutting their

doors. Streets were empty, people stayed inside the walls. How about your area, perhaps the same?

She looked towards the far tree line under bright sunlight and then replied:

-Quieter than before. Most of them own gardens here, so they have to work daily in the morning or afternoon. Are you afraid Tuong?

-Oh ... no, it's nearly deserted here, and the air's so fresh. Does your family grow vegetables around the year?

-Yes, all people here make a living by growing vegetables. But some of my friends were workers in nearby factories

As late afternoon came, south southwest wind got stronger, making tree lines in the middle of the meadow swang their branches likely to play with the flying birds in the sky. Asked Tuong:

-Tham, why you didn't want to work in a factory?

Tham shook her head:

-I like to stay home and help dad. Don't like to work in a factory

He's watching her long, minced hair roll together and flow along the brief wind. The hat that sat on the top of the water pump was blown away and trapped in bunches of vegetables. Tuong ran to pick it up and then gave it back to Tham. He said:

-I must go home now

-Yes, you do

He pointed to the houses in the east:

-How far from here to your home?

-Not far

-So you go first

She smiled at him and then left. Tuong watched Tham wearing her hat walking in the far distance among the gardens and gradually sinking into the dark.

oOo

Tham had picked enough vegetables to cook evening soup. She looked at the quiet trees line under the fading sunlight from the west. She's waiting but Tuong did not appear as two days before. The last people in the meadow already quitting now. She watched thoroughly the faraway corner. Among the darkening gardens, nobody yet stayed after the sun had set down. Tham stood up and went back home with a bunch of vegetables. She's listening to sweety wind ride gently then carry fallen leaves away to nowhere in the east.

    This afternoon Tham's not going to the meadow. In her village, people talked so much about the flu pandemic was spreading in the whole city. In the front yard of her house, bamboo leaves have been dried in thin long branches by hot weather. Anxiously, Tham got out of the house, and stood under trees shade. She watched the vegetable gardens lay side by side and the flock of birds hovering over green plants. Far in the meadow, likely Tuong's walking to the village. Tham got in the house, put on her working dress then quickly moved to see him. Tuong just stopped and seemingly searched for a way. Seeing Tham, he quickly walked towards her.

-Oh, I'm lucky to meet you here. You didn't water vegetables this afternoon?

-Dad did it sooner. Now we go back to over there

She and Tuong moved back to her family garden in the meadow. Some people still working nearby, but they didn't pay attention to them. Tuong said:

-My area was blocked. Just a man living in a mansion be infected. So yesterday I couldn't get here

-My village already got it. People are so afraid. But how could you come to see me while they have blocked the road?

Tuong felt unease for a while and replied:

-Near my home fence there is a drainage running toward the main road. I sneak down there, walk a while then push my body through other underground drainage and finally move out to the meadow

Tham widened her eyes and murmured:

-Does anyone see you?

-The watchmen didn't know that place

Tham smiled:

-Let's wear this old shirt of my father. He often dresses it while working in the garden. Sit down near mine and clear weed, so nobody thinks you're a stranger.

She and Tuong sat in the middle of the garden of Casella alba. He still kept distant space from Tham. But now she is not concerned about it.

-What are people saying in your village?

-Yesterday, some guys carried vegetables through the road near your home, it was blocked. So they knew there was a flu case

-Yes, that man is a foreigner who came back from Europe and has been infected with the flu disease. Then he had to be admitted to an emergency health care center. He was a manager in a factory, living solely in a big house.

Looking at Tuong clearing a thin bunch of weeds around vegetables, Tham smiled. Tuong looked at her:

-Basella alba here is so good

She explained:

-These vegetables must be watered regularly within one week before the whole buyer comes. Do you love Casella alba soup?

-In my family, we often cook Casella alba soup with dried shrimp

-Is there this kind of vegetable in the UK?

Tuong shook the head:

-No, because it's too cold, so they cannot grow up

After clearing wild plants among the vegetable beds, they saw nobody stay in the meadow. The sky was darkening. Tham gave a nice smile to him. They sat together under an eucalyptus tree. Flocks of birds sheltered in the canopy chirping as they had a meeting after a day went out in every corner of the city. Tham asked:

-Have you feared while they blocked your home area?

Tuong nodded:

-The ill man is far from my home, furthermore, he didn't talk to other neighbors. So, everybody feels unworry. I'm bored while staying in one place. It's funny to see you over here. Did anyone in your home ask something?

Tham replied:

-No, several days before my father had seen you here

-Tham, have you often go downtown?

Hesitantly, she held dried melaleuca yellow flowers in the ground and then flew them in the wind. Instead of replying to his question, she said:

-My friends often go together for a few hours and come back

Tuong smiled and watched the distant landscape appear like a painting mixed with violet and orange colors. It's faded and gradually vanishing into a far misty horizon.

oOo

Tham was waiting under the shade of a melaleuca tree. Several tiny flowers from its branches loosen as thin shower into sun rays of the afternoon. She felt a little upset while watching some people still working nearby. Tham calmly cared for some vegetable beds in the garden. The soil under her feet was soft and wet. They have been watered just an hour ago by her father. The familiar sound of steps getting closed. She raised her head to watch. Tuong was standing near a tree, his hands holding a small cat. The large meadow was quiet now. Tham smiled and asked:

-Where do you pick this cat?

-I see it hides in the drainage, so I bring it here. It's too weak, someone left this poor kitty over there

They sat and watched the small cat crawling around Tuong's feet as exploring the new place. She caressed its small head. The kitty murmured a moew meow then raised its tiny paws to fight back. Said Tham:

-Maybe it's hungry

-Yeah, poor cat

-Any pet in your home Tuong?

-Yeah, a dog

-Will you bring this kitty to your home?

-Maybe ... But someone will ask where I pick it up like you

Tham touched the kitty's ears. It swiftly raised fore paws to scratch her. She smiled:

-Does it matter?

-Maybe not, my dog is gentle

-I will give it a name ... Yellow Flowers, ok?

Tuong smiled:

-Yes, any name you like

-I love this name

He took off the sneaker shoes stuck with muddy soil under the sole and put them aside. The green cucumber truss in the far distance looked like long small walls. Some children from distant villages flying kits high in the air over the windy sky. Tuong asked:

-Will someone come here in the evening?

She told him with a nice voice:

-Nobody. I am sending my cell phone number to you. Please call if you want to see me

Tuong took out his fone from his pocket and got them. She looked at the kitty now sitting next to his shoes:

-Could I bring it home?

Tuong thought this was a nice idea. He smiled:

-Yes

oOo

A couple of weeks have passed. The pandemic now wasn't the real fear of people living in Saigon City. Life was revived quietly among houses in the suburbs.

In the dark of the meadow, Tuong sat alone under the melaleuca tree in the middle of the Tham family garden. The bunches of vegetables appeared as misty shapes, then the soft leaves sometimes swung slightly in the wind. Field creatures clang sporadically as a country music band deliberated playing a nocturne song to calm nature. Tham's shade moving through the empty garden towards his place:

-Did you wait so long?

-I just came

She sat beside him. The fresh odors of unknown blossomed flowers in the meadow spread around them and briefly diluted into the air. Tuong said:

-Tomorrow my area will be unblocked. Just a moment when I passed the watched point, nobody in there

-People in my village now hope the pandemic will go far away

Tuong gladly said:

-Maybe ... It will disappear in the coming weeks

Tham gently looking into his eyes:

-When will you be back to school?

Tuong looked into the vast darkness:

-Yes, the college just sends notified mail to students. Next week I will prepare to go back to the UK

He gently held Tham's small soft hand. She trembled a little bit and squeezed his hand:

-What's the season now in the UK?

-Summer just passed. Autumn is going to come. But outside London, there are still beautiful fields, flowers blossom along the roads

Sparkling tiny stars appeared in the sky. There were sounds of flapped wings of some bird scrambling for a place in the branch. The evening air was filled with the odor of basil that just blossomed and flew over in the wind.

-Are there vegetable gardens like my village near your school?

-Yes, in the summer the farms grow vegetables and then supply them to supermarkets and stores. Life in the country is as tranquil as here. I shall take some pictures and send them to you

Tham was watching tiny stars in the west. Next few days, Tuong will say goodbye and leave Saigon. She sadly asked:

-Tuong, would you come back to see me on vacation time?
-Yes, I promise

    In the dark sky, just appeared the winking lights of a plane moving higher and further then disappeared into tranquil space./.

THE LAST TRIP OF THE OLD FISHERMAN

On a dull morning, the old fisherman with gray hair and his boat left the fishing village and sat by a river mouth, where many people had been infected by a mysterious pandemic that quickly killed them.

He then sheltered in a coral island emerged from the sea bed. It was built with white sand following the ocean currents into a treeless sand bar. Then year after year, tiny seeds followed birds and waves stuck there and changed the bare soil into a green lush island floating in the open water.

The day he landed, nobody was there. Just birds making their home and some missing turtles staying to bathe under the sunlight for a while then swimming away.

After towing the thin boat through the white sand beach to the tree shade to avoid the rough sun, he swiftly cleared dead branches and leaves for shelter.

Over here, he thought men didn't need to build homes as inland. So far, the wild nature on this remote island was clean and perfect.

He had left home because he didn't want to be among one of the fishermen killed by this fearful disease. So, he would spend long days here until the pandemic ended. His neighbors were kind guys. Each year, they would meet together to commemorate the victims on sunny days in April.

Three days after the old fisherman had been on the island, a young sailor being dubious about flu ill in a fishing boat was released by his captain on the other side of the island.

The next morning, after hiding food, and drinking water into a bush, the young man was walking around the strange island under fresh sunlight. He got to the other side while the old man was standing under the canopy, watching the sky over the high sea. Surprising by the unwilling encounter, both of them stared at each other without words. Then the young man approached and said:
-Hello, I think there are no people on this island
The old man doubtfully asked:
-Hi, where are you from? How long have you been here?
The young man sadly replied:
-I'm working in a fishing boat. The captain just dropped me on the other side of the island yesterday afternoon
Listening to the strange newcomer, he kept his defending behavior:
-Did they just desert you or somebody?
-Yes, just me

The ocean tide withdrawing from a far distance so the beach likely broadened under the daylight. A flock of seagulls flying and hovering tireless over the immense blue waves stretching to the horizon. The surprising moment went away together with doubtfulness. Said the old fisherman:

-Let's move in and sit under the shade

He's searching for a place on the sand bed by the pile of dead leaves and makes a distance to the old man. Bearing the doomed and desperate mind when being isolated, now he felt not alone despite the old man's distrust. Asked the old man:

-How long will they desert you here?

He shook his head:

-I wouldn't know. Maybe until they think my disease is healed and I am recovered.

The old man asked again:

-Is it flu?

The young man nodded:

-Yes, it is

-How many guys are in the boat?

-Eight

-What do you do in the boat?

-Mechanic

When the old man stopped talking, the young man pointed his finger at the thick bushes in the center of the island and asked:

-Your home is over there?

He replied:

-No, I sailed from an inland village

The young man briefly understood the story. He then asked:

-Is the rogue pandemic raging in your village?

-Yes, three people were buried in the graveyard. This disease was terrible. The sick show themselves pain before dead

-Perhaps for this reason the captain dropped me on this island

The old fisherman watched the young man:

-Have you got a fever or any symptoms?

-For several days, sometimes I've got a fever, headache, and coughing ...
-I've heard villagers whose family members passed away said like this. It's seemingly the first signs of the disease
-Boat guys have given me some drugs
The old shook his head:
-No medicine can cure it

The young man felt desperate. He looked to the open sea and stopped the conversation. The blue color of the sky and the clear water under the strong wings of seagulls were hovering over the pure sunlight that motivated his will to survive. Likely recognizing his heartless words, the old man changed to a gentle tone:
-Come and stay with me. On this shore, the wind is mild and the tide is less strong.
Do you need me to help bring your luggage to this place?
Surprising with the suggestion, the young man replied:
-Thank you, it sounds really good
-Let's go

Not waiting for the young man, the old man jumped up on his feet and then breached through thick bushes. The young man slowly stepped behind. Both of them move under green canopies that hide the sunlight from above. Under their feet were rotten plants laid on the dried sand. Some birds jumped and flew out of nests built in tree branches. They then flapped their wings towards the sound of weaves. After reaching the beach, the old man looked around and waited. The young man stepped out of the tree lines pointed his finger to the right side:

-I dropped off my baggage over here

Leading the old man to the spot, he pulled the thick branches covered by liana outside. There were two dark green sacks and two freshwater plastic containers.

-You carry this small one. I take the plastic containers and the other sack

Tossing the sack to his shoulder, the old man asked:

-Hey, I do not know your name

-Sorry, my name is Mat

The old man held the sack in his shoulder with one hand, the other grabbed the handle of a plastic container, and then he walked back into the bushes. The young hesitated to leave but was confused and looking at the other container. The loud voice of the old man resounds within the leaves:

-Leave it over there. Will pick it up in another time

A few minutes later, the ardent voice of the old man called:

-Now, quickly move out

He feels tired but tries to follow the traces of feet on the sand floor. The old man's kindness and his sturdy body pushed him out of the sadness and worry of a prisoner who deserted on an empty island.

Back to the boat, he watched the old man cutting branches to build another shelter in a hiding place. When the young man walked nearer, the old man said:

-You would rest here, it's less wind than outside

After work was done, he climbed onto the boat and threw out an old mat. Then brought it to the new hut and spreading on the sand floor.

-Thank you

The young man sat down and drank water. The old man took out stuff inside two sacks and then put it on the sand. About several dozen instant noodle packs, rice boxes, canned foods, salty spices, an old aluminum cooker ... The rest included clothes, a medicine box, a kitchen knife, a plastic cup, and some more dried stuff wrapped in anti-moisture sheets. He briefly reckoned that, with this stuff, a man could survive more than a dozen days without anxiety. He handled all things back into the sacks then stood up and put them to the boat. He watched the young man whose name was Mat, close his eyes and lie with the unwell face. Then he took the fishing line roll and walked to the shore. The young man woke up and asked:

-What's your name?

Heard the sudden voice, the old man turned back to watch and replied:

-Cat ... Now I go catching some fish

Picked up and cut a snail into pieces for bait, the old man moved out and stood among the waves and threw the line into far water then slowly rolled it back on a round stick. As the sun went higher in the sky, strong winds pushed the tide to the island. The crashed waves soaked his T-shirt and shorts. When hooking a fish, he drew it to the shore. When the sun rose into mid-sky, he left the fierce sea waves, walked back to the beach, and began cooking.

The old man made a fire from three dead branches and cooked lunch. Bunches of smoke rose to canopies. Moments later, the wind swept them away to the high sea. By the prow, Mat was sleeping on the mat. His body suddenly moved and stretching his legs then raised his head towards the bright fire. A string of three fish is speared on a bamboo stick and roasted over a smoky fire hole near the rice cooker. Seemingly the fever was raging in his body. Old Cat sat attentively to rotating fishes over a fire. The black wet T-shirt clung to a tree branch and flew like a sea pirate's flag. The rice and fish were well done. He woke Mat up:

-Meal time now

Mat opened his tired eyes and sat up. The rice cooker sat between them, near a dish of roasted fish, with a bit of fish sauce and decorated by a pinch of dried chili powder. Old Cat sat barely on the sand. He held a rice bowl while watching Mat. Mat scooped rice into half a bowl and ate it with a piece of fish. Watching Mat hardly swallow some pieces of food, the old man's voice inserted among rustling sea waves sounds:

-Can you eat?

Mat just nodded his head while chewing. The waves moved by the beach then crashed into white tiny foams and burst under the sunlight. Wind, sun, trees, sand, water ... on this island were as pure as the beginning day of earth. The bad fever drove him dizzy and stole away his appetite. Conversely, the old man ate as well as a young fisherman. After the meal, he took care of nothing, just lying on the old mat under the canopy decorated with thick green leaves.

    Trying to consume the last grains of rice, Mat brought bowls and dishes to clean by the seashore and then dried them up in the boat. He watched his sack still lying by the old sail. In a far corner under the shade, old Cat slept without worry. Mat went back to the canopy, built a small dune as a pillow, and laid down then tried to rest. On the beach, the tide reached its highest level. Strong wind and waves were softening and started setting back. After lunch, Mat took a deep breath and inhaled pure and salty air into his lungs. His ill body felt better for the first time on this quiet shore. He looked to the old Cat with a grateful mind.

    Afternoon falling, the sun moved to the other side of the island. The old man woke up in the calm air. He drank some water and then stayed in the tree shade watching to high sea. The tide had withdrawn and left some plastic bottles, and old fishing nets with buoys painted the number of an unknown boat tangled to rotten logs laid among leaves from mangrove woods.

Watching the sick young man sleeping near the boat, he recalled sometimes he had sailed here and stayed alone for several days. He was the only person who randomly visited the sandy island. The others discovered nothing precious over here so they didn't waste time to ransack. This time, the fearful pandemic pressed the unknown boatmen to send him and this island a patient. Though he was old, still be frightened by this deadly disease. Just not the others.

Walking towards the boat, he picked the fishing line, gathered some snails on the beach, and cut them for bait. By naked feet, the old man stepped towards the waves. There were plenty of fish and shrimp swimming around the remoted island. Spent half an hour fishing in sea waves, he brought a bunch of fish to the seashore and put them near the fire hole. As the sky was still bright, he cut through the island to the other shore where the young man landed yesterday. He watched the large sandy beach running along the tree line, nothing changed. He took the water can hid under a bush then walked back. The young man leaned his back to a tree trunk. His exhausted eyes looked to the sea, then slowly moved toward the old man who just appeared under the canopies.

Old Cat built a fire. Smoke was spreading from dead branches and then burned into strong fire. The red flame rises under two cookers' bottoms. As usual, in the evening, whether at home or on the island, he cooked some extra food for tomorrow. When boiling fish was done, he took them to the dish to cool down., then added some fish sauce and a bit of dry chili powder. The rice was also cooked. Falling asleep for a while, Mat opened his eyes. Old Cat gently asked:

-You still have a fever?

He nodded and drank some fresh water. Said the old man:

-Rice and fish are cooked. Eat whenever you like

Sat under the canopy, old Cat ate a piece of boiled fish. His eyes randomly looked far away where high waves rippling under the hovering wings of large sea birds. A big commercial vessel painted white and black cruised slowly near the island to the northeast and left behind thin gray smoke. When scooping more rice into the cooker, he then watched the young man. Likely, he now looking better. But still leaning to the tree. He said:
-Eat more fish, this afternoon I caught a lot

He nodded, slowly stood up, and had dinner. Later noon was coming. Following strong waves, sea tides rise higher. Fierce winds blew over hours and violently shook trees and canopies until the sun went down in the west.

After the meal, the old man took a long walk along the beach and then came back.

The first evening while the young man has been on the island gradually falls. Old Cat threw some branches of smoldering charcoal into the fire hole that billowed thin smoke. A few minutes later, with the help of the wind, they burst into flames and shed bright light on the beach. Then he rested on his mat. Under canopies, Mat lay quietly on the sand with arms crossed beneath his head. The sky disappeared in the dark. The small island seemingly sank into the vast ocean floor.

oOo

Old Cat lunched alone then took a short nap to evade the hot sun. Being wake up by the strong wind sweeping over bushes, he found a knife in the boat and then chopped some branches to erect two small walls to shield the hidden hut of Mat.

Drinking some water in the cup, the old man handed the fishing line to the shore. As usual, he tried to catch some fish for dinner. The hat hid almost half over his face, just the long brown hair exposed in the neck. His tanned skin was exposed to the sunlight. Wind blowing rudely from high sea to island. When hooked enough fish, he walked back under canopies.

This evening he would cook porridge with fish for young patients. When tides struck rogue waves to the shore, the young man was wakened by loud noise and opened his eyes. The porridge was cooked and ready to serve him. Mat ate a full porridge bowl. Old Cat found a silent joy inside him. He knew the young strength dwelling within Mat's strong body was struggling. The patient would survive until the boat turned back to pick him up.

oOo

The young sailor lay motionless in his corner until the 7th day. Then he began to regain his health. Old Cat's stuff which was brought from inland just dried up. They now cooked foods from the sacks that had been left on the beach for Mat.

Night falling, the old man sat on the sand by the whole fire shedding warm light under the dark quiet sky. Recalling the shore on the other side of the island, he stood up and made a round walk. Finally, he ended a day when turning at the same place. Watched the young man in a dark corner with a swift look, and he went back to his corner and rested.

Under the canopies, he thinks about the life and death cycle circling human life. From youth time to weakened age. People didn't earn the same destiny. Some died too soon and, left behind broken hearts of lovers. Some lived a hundred years and stood steadily as sturdy old trees on a high mountain. But the God of Death never missed any soul.

Mat crossed the sand beach and stood by Old Cat fishing among waves submerging to his knees. Under the morning sunlight, the water was so clear, that he could see white sand on the sea floor. Old Cat slowly rewound the line into a branch. Being hooked, the fish was struggling when exposed to swallow water. Unhooked fish from the line, he cast it to the shore and handed the line to Mat:
-Add more bait and cast it far away in the water, then slowly retrieving to check some more.

Back to the shore, he sat under the shade. Mat standing in the water, casted the line to far distance and looked at it sinking under waves. Fresh and clean air likely made him forget the disease that he had suffered several days ago. Waiting for a while, the line drifting to and fro then slightly stretching outwards. Maybe some fish snatched baits. He rolled it up and moved back to the shore. Some more fish were hooked for a lunch meal.

In the evening, after having a good meal, they sit on the sand by hot bright flames. Mat said:
-Maybe in the next few days, the boat will pick me up
Said Old Cat:
-If the captain had said so. Sure, they would sail back in the coming days
-How long would you stay on this island?
-The kinds of stuff that I carry along enough for half a month
He doubted Old Cat's answer:
-You didn't bring fresh water

-In the middle of the wood, there is a small water source that can produce a dozen liters, enough for one man's daily needs. If the boat won't be back, so what do you do?

Taking a brief thinking, Mat insisted:

-Surely, they will

Old Cat asked:

-You got married, did you?

-I've not yet married. After this trip, I plan to have a family and move to the mainland then seeking another job

-So now you're living on an island?

-Indeed, my island is located in the southwest of this one. Cat, do you know it?

The old fisherman nodded:

-Some fishermen in my village have told me about it. But I've never been there before

Mat asked:

-Your boat moves both by engine and sail, doesn't it?

-Yes, both. The boat where you had sailed that ran by a big strong engine?

-That's right. At present, most fishing boats go farther in open seas. So they need the big one
Old Cat stood up:
-I'm going to walk around the island. Would you?
Mat shook his head. His eyes were shone by red flames swinging with the sea wind.

Mat didn't like it. He sat near the fire hole. Tide rising in the immense dark changing the sea current into black color. Strong wind swept over bushes, pushing their leaves to the same side. He watched the high sea, wishing a boat would appear by the shore that shone by a big fire.

oOo

Days passed but there were no boats to come. Foods were almost depleted. Old Cat said:
-Perhaps they don't come to pick you up as promised due to some reasons. I must go back to inland to scout the news. Would you go with me?
Hesitating for some minutes, Mat replied:
-I deeply want to go back home and see my relatives

-If I leave, there are no stuffs for you here

Everything seemingly stuck to a dead end. Mat sadly sat with his head down between knees. The T-shirt that wore over his neck was blown away and floating on the water. But he was still motionless. Old Cat brought it back and putting near Mat's foot. Then said:
-May I sail you home by my boat, young man!
Mat raised up his face with little hope:
-Thank you

The next morning, Old Cat and Mat checked the engine, sail pole, and fuel tank. When the tide rose higher, they pushed the boat into seawater then started the engine and moved out. After sailing several times around the island, the boat is anchored next to the sand tip. Now they tried to hook some fish for a meal.
-Sailing from here to your home will take half a day. Do you think the engine is in good condition – Old Cat asked
-It's old. I fear for your trip back to here
-If it breaks down, I'll use sails
Mat said with confidence:

-It doesn't matter. When we get to my island, I'll fix it and refuel the tank
Old Cat smiles:
-Tomorrow morning we'll depart

Mat watching the fishing line sinking into the sea floor. Sitting on the boat, he looked at the green trees lining on tiny island that emerged lonely on the sea. Fishing for a while, they had some big fish. The sun moving high in the middle of the sky. After hooking some more fish, Old Cat said:
-It's enough. We have to sail back

Mat lifted the anchor and helped to tie the sails. Windswept hardly. The old sails were inflated and drove the boat slowly moving on waves. On the stern, Old Cat drove it to the open water, then made one more trip around the island. Finally, they stopped and docked near the shore.

Mat felt delightful. Old Cat silently walked to his corner under the shade. The young man built fire from hot coal and cooking.

The next morning, when the tide began to withdraw, Old Cat and Mat started the boat engine and moved to the open water. They would soon depart to the southwest. Luckily, the boat was getting tailwind. Old Cat steered it on the calm grey water then handled the wheel to the young man. The sun slowly rose and shone in their backward. Old Cat sat and ate a rice bowl with the fried fish of yesterday. Then he went back to his seat and took Mat's duty. Mat leaning back the pole. He was inspired when recalling the coconut tree line under the mountain ridge that he would see again. The boat was sailing a very long way in the void water. Just seagulls hovering above the blue sky. Then suddenly, the engine slowed down and stopped. Mat looked to the fuel tank and said:

-It's nearly empty

They lifted a big sail to the peak of the wooden pole. The boat starts sailing again on the sea. The current changed its way under the strong wind. The boat had to make a zigzag moving under the ingenious hands of Old Cat.

The sky gradually darkened around them. The evening was falling in the west. The sun almost disappeared into thick clouds. People can feel the unpredictable weather would fill the empty sea. The southern corner's getting darker. Mat and Old Cat both worried as the wind and waves grew stronger. The boat moved like a leaf as the old sail was rudely inflated. Some lightning struck down from a black cloud as they wanted to chop the sky into two parts. A typhoon unexpectedly appeared then rocking the boat under a fearful tropical rain. Unexpectedly, the big sail was torn down as an old paper. The boat now running as a wild horse and drifting out of Old Cat's hands. It was surrounded and crushed under giant waves. Some moments later, they quickly sank to the depth.

The next morning, a fishing boat found Mat gripping an empty plastic container after hours floating in the water. Unfortunately, nobody saw the old fisherman and the boat. Perhaps everything had vanished into the ocean floor.

Each year, Mat sent flowers to the sea to commemorate the day the old fisherman and his boat were sunk by a cruel storm. He would never miss the good brave old man who had sailed him back home./.

THE MAN WHO SAW THE ANGEL

Mr. Bin sat on the saddle of his bicycle and drove slowly on a winding dirt road to the north of the highland town. As autumn comes, cool air covers the lush green landscape of the mountains under a blueish sky. The old mountain man was cycling, and thinking about the pink-white flowers that Y Minh, his granddaughter wanted to have a few branches, even though she didn't know the name. It seemed that Y Minh would give these flowers to someone, but she didn't want to tell him yet. Maybe that person was probably a woman. Mr. Bin struggled to ride up the hillside in front of him. The sound of gravel and dirt splashing from the wheels hitting the mud fenders resounded in the deserted field. When crossing the low hill, he saw the dark brown tiled roof of the nuns' monastery appearing lonely in the valley. He hoped to ask them for some of those beautiful flowers even though he didn't know anyone there.

The reason he knew this remote place outside the town that went a few months ago when riding by the monastery, he had seen white-pink flowers blooming in the yard.

The image of beautiful flowers and his granddaughter gives him more power. Mr. Bin pushed his feet hard to make the bike move quickly by the vegetable gardens. Arriving at the monastery, he stopped in front of a closed wooden gate. No one was in the front yard. He slowly down the bike on the grass, then leaned back against the tree outside the monastery. The afternoon sunlight shone over the grassland with yellow thin rays. Under the tree shade, the old man closed his eyes to find a sleep in the silence. In his small dream, he saw a young woman dressed in a blue "ao dai" like clouds color in the high sky gently shaking his shoulder and asking:

-Who are you looking for?

At the same moment, the sound of footsteps walking on gravelly soil rustling. He opened his eyes and jumped up. Looking at the young girl with a gentle, smiling oval face, he waited silently. The girl asked with kindness:

-Did you come to the monastery to find someone or something?

After an amazed moment, suddenly feeling embarrassed for oversleeping, he replied:

- I'm not looking for anyone, I just want to ask for some flowers - he looked at the opening gate and asked more - did you come from there?

The girl still kept her smile and nodded:

-Yes, I am

He told the young girl about his intentions:

-I have a nine-year-old granddaughter who wants flowers grown in this yard to give to someone

-Yes, but the monastery has a lot of flowers...

Thinking then sitting on the ground. A moment later, he stood up, smiled, and replied with a simple and bewildered look:

-White flowers with a bit of rosy color

- Please wait here

He stood near the gates watching the young girl turn around and enter the monastery yard in a happy mood. A moment later, returning with a small bouquet of white-pink flowers, she gently gave it to him.

-Thank you very much - Mr. Bin said

    The girl smiled and bowed, then walked in, closed the gate, and disappeared into the quiet afternoon shadow of the garden. He looked over the fence again, then placed the bouquet in the square iron basket in front of the handlebars, then got on the saddle and left.

    Under the gentle sunny sky, the sound of the monastery bell reminds the evening prayer session spreading across the fields. Smiles on his face, Mr. Bin felt overjoyed as he rode back to town. His old legs were tired when the bike moved up and downhill roads. But he returned with beautiful flowers thanks to the kindness of the young girl in the monastery. In his mind, it was a miracle.

Coming home from school in the afternoon, Y Minh happily handled the bouquet in her hand. The granddaughter came and whispered to him:
-You know, Grandpa, today is Mom's birthday. Later, I will give this nice bouquet to my mother

The grandchild surprised him. The constant war has forced his family to leave the village and settle home here and there. He no longer remembered his daughter's birthday. Suppressing emotions, his tears waiting to fall. He smiled and said:
- Y Minh is so good. It's been many years, and I had forgotten
-Mom said, now grandpa is old and often forgets. From now on, every year I will remember everyone's birthday in the house
She came and sat next to him, telling him what the teacher at school had said:

-Each person's date of birth is very important. That is when God plants a new seed on the earth. Instead of growing as a tiny tree in the forest, each seed miraculously grows into a human being.

Y Minh also said that each person has a heart, not a place to harbor hatred but to love each other. The granddaughter picked up her small bouquet and put it on the table. He tiredly leaned his back against the wall and closed his eyes.

Sure enough, in the afternoon, when Y Minh handed a nice bouquet for her birthday before a meal, his daughter said in surprise:
-God, thank you so much. Where are the flowers so beautiful?
Y Minh excitedly said:
-Grandpa picked it

The daughter smiled at him for a long time as if expressing her thanks. Sitting nearby, he silently looked at the little happy shadow just appearing from the flowers. The evening became an amazing moment when everyone sat around the dinner in the warm stilt house. His amnesia was temporarily pushed into a corner to make room for old memories. Mr. Bin felt there were stones lighting up in his head. His brain was so old, it was gradually rejecting the living things in the small world of the town.

oOo

A week later, Mr. Bin took the bike out of the house in the morning. He wanted to go somewhere, so he sat on the saddle and slowly rode through the empty road to the north.

Passing the small houses along the road, a highland scene appears. In front of his eyes were dirt roads spreading around the town, basking in the sunlight.

The bike took him through successive fields on undulating hills. Suddenly he wanted to stop in front of the monastery. His memory still retained the image of colorful flowers behind two brown gates. Gently dropping the bike onto the grass, he sat under a tree looking blankly at the fields. In the morning, the wind whispers through the tranquil hills. The blue sky was decorated by white clouds floating like thin cotton balls. The red dirt road winding up and down far to the north as a long thread leading him to the village on a remote hill surrounded by green forests to the west. He closed his eyes for a long time and tried to remember it. That place was like a dream that sometimes disappeared and then reappeared. He had to close his eyes tightly to ensure that familiar images would not escape from the two small black round boxes. A moment later, he laid down on the grass in the shade and slept soundly.

When suddenly woke up, he looked at the sky was filled with gray clouds. Signs of rain were about to fall around town. Behind him, the two monastery gates were still closed. He brought up the bike. Someone put a small bouquet in the basket. Looking at the bouquet without blinking, and then turning their eyes to the monastery yard. He whispered and bowed his head before leaving.

Before he got into the town, a thunderstorm broke out, pouring hard rains on the fields and houses on the road. But he kept riding slowly under a strong wind likely to blow everything into the sky. He feared the bouquet would be rolled away, so he bent down and held it when riding. In the afternoon, Y Minh held a bouquet and asked him:

-Who gave Grandpa these flowers?

Unknown who picked the flowers for him. The old man's mind just remembered two brown gates, he replied:

-In the monastery

oOo

The following week he went northward again. The bike and he rode on the familiar road leading to the old village. Passed by the monastery, he did not stop. All his strength now putting on the pedal to ride forward. Going far away from the monastery, houses, and fields gradually disappeared, only rocks and bushes. The wild green color of the mountains awakened nature's strong love in his heart and muscles, driving him to overcome the long road ahead. Finally, there was a steep hill slope before he reached the desired destination. Moving bike past the empty stilt houses, he looked around. He vaguely realized decay and desolation were residing here. A small old woman standing at the stair base of a stilt house calls his name. Her face and both hands were deformed by leprosy. He stopped but was bewildered and didn't realize who she was.

Hesitantly looking at the poor woman and the house for a while, he walked to the road end of the village where just a trace of path crawling among the grasses towards the distant mountains. Nothing left to explore, Mr. Bin stood hesitantly for a few seconds and then returned to the old woman. But no one was there anymore. With a bit of sadness on his face, he rode the bike out of the village. From the high slope, his bike moved faster and faster on the dirt and gravel road. The green trees on both sides rushed backward as they were chasing each other. Just reaching the end of the hill slope, he and the bike fell flat on the ground. Sitting up with a sharp pain all over his body, his left arm was scratched with a long cut with red blood. He picked up the slipper that fell next to him and put it back on his feet, his ears listening to the sounds of the forest leaves rustling in the wind. From afar, two women on two bicycles were approaching. When the two had to stop because the bike was blocking the road. He watched the nun and the young girl parking their bikes under the tree shade. The nun came closer and looked at the broken and bleeding elbow and said:

-He's injured

The young girl said:

-Sister, let me bandage it for him

She took a first aid box from her bag and began to wipe away the dirt, and blood from on his arm, then bandaged the wound. Now he felt better, the pain almost went away. The girl looked at him with nice eyes:

-Are you going to visit your old village?

He bowed his head. The nun asked:

-Do you know this man?

-Yes, sometimes when I came home from school, I saw him asleep under the tree shade in front of the monastery. One time, he asked for some flowers in the yard and then went home. I thought he was a bit dementia. But it's too far for him to ride here today

He recognized the young girl and immediately said:

-Visit the old village... Thank you

The nun smiled:

-Yes, let's go home, ride carefully so you don't fall

The girl brought up the bike and handed it into his hands. He looked at the gentle black eyes under the hat and said:

-Thank you

He got on the saddle and started pedaling slowly. The nun and the girl watched for a while then led their bikes up the hill slope. Every week they rode here to care for some leprosy patients who were still dwelling in this remote village.

oOo

Since that accident, he has never ridden out of town again. As aging, his health gradually weakens. Over the years, his dementia gradually erased the memories that were as faint as thin mist in his head.

The following winter, a serious illness left him in bed. His joy now was his granddaughter often came to talk, even though everything was no longer as clear as when he was a healthy man.

One Sunday afternoon, returning from church, Y Minh sat and drew on a piece of paper, and then brought it to show him. She smiled brightly:
-Grandpa, I drew an angel that looks like the singing teacher at church

He watched the image of a girl owned wings on her shoulders, holding a bouquet in both hands and smiling with him. The granddaughter continued:
-Grandpa, was my drawing angel beautiful?
 He smiled and nodded. Y Minh asked again:
-Have you ever seen an angel?
This time he replied with a fainted voice:
-Yes... I had seen an angel in front of the monastery gate

Y Minh smiled and looked at him with widened eyes. She went to her mother was cooking and whispered:

-Grandfather said there was an angel at the gate of the monastery. Is that true, mother?

The daughter looked at his eyes just closed and said:

-Yes, grandfather had seen the angel there

The next day he died when the war just ended. No more gun sounds in the night.

The hilly land around the small town on the plateau gained back its quiet and peaceful like a few decades ago.

His grave was built within the cemetery fence of the mountain parish outside the town.

His granddaughter has planted around it some colorful flowers that grow together with nameless wild plants./.

THE SWEET POTATO ISLET

After long heavy rains poured down on the upper streams in September, the flooding water containing muddy silt from the Cambodian border appeared as a great army rushed to the Mekong delta rivers of Viet Nam. A vast sea of fresh water stretched from the Tien river connecting to the Hau River. Then a few months later, the flood escaped to the East Sea and Thailand Bay through both estuaries and canals.

When the dry season turned back, on a remote river in Dong Thap near the border, a small islet emerged from the water near the confluence. Swiftly, when the islet has been dried under warm tropical sunlight, thousands of tiny seeds follow the current and cling to the new islet. All of them began to germinate, rooted in fertile soil. Quickly, the young plants started to rise and grow into green bushes next to swathes of young reeds have were waving under the wind.

Some more weeks passed, and when the brown silt layer got drier, from downstream a small junk with a thatched roof of monk Nam Khien, aged 40, docked by the young trees on the river bank. A bamboo pole was plunged into the river. The junk sat motionless there the whole morning.

Midafternoon, the monk moved out of the roof and watched the wild plants on the islet. His eyes saw the tranquil landscape of the border. He stepped down to the dry bank and walked to the west side of the islet, stood near the edge of the water, and looked to the river that flowed from the remote wood in the northwest. Then he went back to the junk.

After a while, some smoke rose high to the blue quiet sky from the thatched roof. Cooking done, he sat in the stern and had dinner. His small eyes sometimes watched the sky, then looked down to the river as if he tried to foresee the weather. His short beard and long black hair plus his thin face together make him a good-natured man. The evening has just come, monk Nam Khien handled a bamboo stick then stepped down and hammered it to the river bank carefully before tying it to the junk by a rope.

Shortly, the dark sank all things into deep black night. A fire flashed in the middle of the islet shone the monk brought some kind of stuff to the bank. That night he carried a sleeping bag to the islet. Stars appeared in the clear summer sky and twinkled on the top of trees lined along the bank. On the river, the currents sometimes flowed quickly, making small waves twinkle under stars light. At last, everything likely had sunk deep into the water and left no signs behind.

The next morning, the monk woke up early and then rowed the junk to a river branch that went deep into the mangrove forest of Dong Thap Muoi marsh. The junk passed some thatched houses sat on a high ground. Nearby, some junks sat under tamanu and melaleuca trees shade. He crossed a large swamp that flourished with numberless nenuphars and lotus flowers then stopped near the wood. From the junk stern, his small black eyes watched the vast landscape. In this wild land, there's no house and no people, just trees, bushes, and wild grasses growing far out to the horizon. Just found some high melaleuca trees, he jumped into shallow water, chopped some, and put them into the junk bed. Need some more things to build the roof, Nam Khien rowed deeper into a small canal and moved next to green nipa palm trees, then he chopped big leaves and put them on top of trunks. The junk's overloaded, and he rowed back to the islet.

From the morning till late afternoon, the monk built a sparse cabin on stilts in the middle of the islet. As there was shelter from rain and sunlight, he carried his small property from the junk to the cabin and then had a bath in the river. Perhaps monk Nam Khien had found a good place, so he planned to live long years in this new islet.

In the night, a big fire flared into the sky. The small islet shone as a lighthouse at the confluence.

Monk Nam Khien began to hoe the land on the islet to grow sweet potatoes. He only left a strip of land near the bank to grow gourds, and cucumbers near the bamboo truss.

When having spare time, the monk rowed the junk to a remote canal for fishing and picking up wild vegetables. His life was as simple as a bird in the mangrove wood.

In a late afternoon, two strange men sitting in a junk appeared when monk Nam Khien brought water from the river to irrigate the sweet potato field. They came from downstream and rowed nearer when they saw a man in the islet. The older sat in front of the junk and asked:

-My home sits by the canal that runs through the woods. Do you just come here?

-Yes, right

-My name is Sau Tung. Behind is my brother, his name's Bay Tung

Monk Nam Khien nodded and greeted two strange men. Saw their gentle behavior, he replied:

-I'm Nam Khien, seeking this desolated islet with fertile soil, so I grow some sweet potatoes. Come to my cabin for some drinks, please

Sau Tung brothers stuck the pole to the bank then stepped down and followed Nam Khien to his cabin in the middle of the field. The monk poured water from a smoky kettle into two old clay bowls and then put them on the floor made of melaleuca tree trunks. Drinking over half the bowl, Sau Tung looks at the monk:

-Where was your hometown before you came here?

The monk answered with an ambiguous explanation:

-Previously, I'd lived on an islet located in Hau River

Sau Tung said:

-We've lived in this field for around three years

-Yes ... I knew that place

Bay Tung doubtfully asked:

-Brother Nam, do you live alone here?

The monk nodded gently:

-I have no wife, no family

Seeing the sweet potato sprouts in the field, said Bay Tung:

-The land here is fertile, potatoes will give good yield. We had to go now, brother Nam. When you have spare time, let's visit our home and other neighbors. It's late, we go home, Sau Nam Khien said softly:

-Thank you

He led two men towards the river bank. Sau Tung jumped onto the junk and released the pole. He friendly said:

-Bye, I go home

The junk moved against the current to the upper stream and then turned to a small canal hidden by wild plants that grew along the bank. The monk continued his work by irrigating the rest of the potato field to the end before break. While having a bath on the river, he caught some snails as baits for night and morning fishing.

The meeting with two men who lived in a lonely village near the woods didn't make Nam Khien feel upset or happy either. For more than a dozen years now, he often lived far away from villages and self-managed to survive. He and his junk used to move everywhere in the delta.

The next day, in the shining mid-noon, a couple who looked older than Sau Tung rowed their junk to the islet while the monk cooked lunch. They stood in front of the cabin and greeted:

-Hi brother Nam Khien, we're living near the Sau Tung brothers' houses. He told us yesterday they've visited the islet. Thus, this morning we come to see you.

Monk Nam Khien smiled, and handled the kettle and glass while standing near the door:

-Please come in and have a seat

The man got a sturdy body, with an opened mind and a round face, said:

-Thanks, I'm Ba Moi, my wife is Sau brothers' cousin. Just heard they said you are alone here. If you need something, please let me know …

The monk bowed his head to thank his generous mind:

-Thank you. Likely I've just come here for one month

They don't enter the cabin. The woman looks around and then comments:

-Our family has been here for three years. When rowing along this river in the dry season, we could see a little sand bar. But in the rainy season, the river goes immensely. This year the grand river had sent plenty of silt and mud here, and the islet has grown quickly. New fertile soil is good for everything.

Ba Moi handed the local tobacco on a coarse paper and asked:

-Brother Nam, do you smoke?

Monk Nam Khien shook his head:

-No thanks, I don't smoke

He rolled up a cigarette, lit it then smoked and breathed out small smokes:

-We go now. When you row next to our home, let's visit me and Sau Tung. Every person has heard your name already

The monk the man and his wife walked to the junk. Under the bright sunlight, the Ba Moi couple rowed away. In the noon, the wind was blowing from the woods creating tiny waves rippling on the river. The blue sky seemingly overwhelmed the river and reed field that stretched to faraway swamps.

oOo

Three months later, Nam Khien harvested the first sweet potato crop that burst a corner of the cabin. The monk donated a part to Sau Tung's villagers. Growing in fertile soil, the sweet potatoes got really good taste.

Some days after, monk Nam Khien began to hoe the soil for another crop. He tried to avoid the net flooding season. The mild weather of the delta offered a peaceful life on the islet. Sau Tung brothers, and Ba Moi couple often visited and talked or gave him fish, some rice together with wild vegetables, or a bunch of firewood.

oOo

The dry season lengthened over May then white clouds appeared over the whole delta. Signs that the weather was going to change. Big swathes of clouds have followed the southwest wind and wandered over rivers, canals, fields, and swamps. In the islet, monk Nam Khien was going to harvest another crop.

After lots of rain had poured down, the small green canals, and creeks flowed from Dong Thap Muoi within months now changed into murky water. The islet turned into a thick and sticky muddy ground. After another good harvest, more potatoes have been filled the small cabin.

Two months later, the rivers on the upper stream next to the border rose higher. Sau Tung and Ba Moi rowed to the islet. They helped the monk to strengthen his cabin against the flood. However, they still worried about the lone cabin sitting near the confluence, where floods run across the border and often overflew the bank each year. Everybody wanted Monk Nam Khien to move to the village for some months while the islet was surrounded by water. But he said this up to the situation. He will move to the Sau Tung brothers' home when needed.

Towards the year's end, after long heavy rains, the river slowly reached the cabin floor. The monk moved potatoes and tools to a higher place under the roof. Daily he still cooked on the stove as before. Sometimes strong wind thrusted violently across the confluence, the cabin slightly twisted and trembled likely it's going to be tossed away.

oOo

Undergone the stormy and rainy season, in the small village of Ba Tung, where seven stilt houses were sitting on the high ground that about the size of half a football yard emerged in the middle of the water. Every day, village people rowed to the wild field to fish and pick up vegetables. When the weather was cloudy and raining, the monk and other villagers enjoyed spare time. They often gathered at the Ba Tung brother's or Ba Moi's house. Men smoked cigarettes, talked, ate, or drank local spirits with dried fish. Far away near the tree lines bobbing up and down in the water, some boats moved swiftly across the submerged fields and disappeared into the horizon. Sau Tung brandished his hand towards these boats and said:

-These smugglers go to Cambodia and then trafficking goods. They do it when waters overflow the border until the lunar new year.

Some smugglers used to visit the high-ground village. This year, when their boats moved nearer, the man standing in the stern raised his hand to Sau Tung, Bay Tung making mysterious signs. Big surprise when seeing a stranger, they stared at the monk and then sped up the boat on vast murky water under a dull sky.

One afternoon after picking up vegetables from the swarm, monk Nam Khien rowed back the junk across the village, Bay Tung waved his hand to him:

-Brother Nam, come here

The junk's gliding on the water next to the stilt house:

-What's the matter brother?

-A moment ago, two rangers came and asked me:

- What is that cabin sitting at the confluence and nobody inside?

I said:

- That's yours. Maybe he rowed to fish in the swamp

-Did they tell anything more?

-No, perhaps they're afraid people from across the border build it, that can cause some trouble over here

Monk Nam Khien replied with happiness:

-Thank you so much. I've rowed to the swamp and gathered some vegetables. Bye

Last months before year-end, when the flood withdrew, the islet emerged again near the confluence. Had stayed many weeks tranquil under the water, the islet reinforced by a thick layer of silt and mud, so now it grew bigger and higher. When the soil went drier and thicker, the monks started to hoe and then make beds for sweet potato crops as last year.

One mid-noon, after a meal, Nam Khien's leaning back to the cabin wall to watch reed fields across the river. Summer light shone far away in the delta. Wild plants regained their colors and grew strongly over the swamps. Suddenly, in this delightful scene, monk Nam Khien heard some voices sounded from confluence into the islet:

-Help, someone help us please … Help … Help

Monk Nam Khien stood up and walked to the rear side of his cabin. Two women were clinging to a capsized junk floating from a river across the border. Saw his appearance, the young woman raised her hand repeatedly and then shouted:

-Please help us, brother

Getting confused for a brief moment then seeing his junk, monk Nam Khien moved to the river bank and released the rope. He rowed quickly towards those women. They're slowly flowing through the confluence to the big river. His junk rowed for a while then caught up the victims. He said to the young one:

-Bring your mother first onto the junk

The monk holds the arm of the soaked gray-haired old woman, soared with water and fear into the junk. She's blind so she'd to creep in and rest under the roof. The young woman pointed her hand to the capsized junk:

-Please help to capture my clothes basket

-You come up here and steer the junk, so I can take it back

Monk Nam Khien grabbed the victim's hand and pulled her out of the water. Then he swam next to her junk and said:

-Give me the rope to tie it

Taking the rope from her hand, the monk tied it to the junk then swam and took back her clothes bag which floating nearby. After turning the capsized junk and bailing out water, the monk climbed back on the junk and said:

-You sit and row from the stem Monk Nam Khien and the young woman rowed with all effort. They got the islet, and the junk slowly sat by the bank. After docking, the monk watched the young woman, aged between 25 to 30 years old. She guided her gray-haired mother and walked to the stem. Guessing she was blind, Nam Khien got nearer then holding her hands, and stepped down to the islet. Quietly he walked towards the cabin. The women's clothes were wet now. Nam Khien handed them his old brown dress and a khaki. Then he stepped out and closed the door. Waiting quite long after they've dressed already, the monk quietly opened the door and gave them boiling sweet potatoes from the cooker:

-Please serve yourselves, and drinking water is in the kettle

Then he pointed to the pole stretching over the stove:

-Dry your wet clothes in there

The sky was still shining, monk Nam Khien rowed to the swamps for fishing. When the sun set down on the reed field, he rowed back and cooked the evening meal. After dinner, Nam Khien sat and rested in front of the cabin. When the night was falling, he got in and lit up the candle to shine inside then got out. Two women stayed motionless in a corner. Sitting outside in the dark, the monk thought about tomorrow. Surely after recovery, these women will go back to their homes. So, he needn't ask them more. Tonight, the small cabin's enough room for three people. The tiny sound of steps moving toward the door. In the dark, monk Nam Khien is listening. The young woman timidly appeared by the threshold and said:

-Mister ...

-Yes, what's the matter?

She said softly:

-Yes, my name is Nhieu. Anyway, we'd like to show our gratitude to you. And you

-My name's Nam Khien

-I'd like to tell this story to you, brother Nam. My family was overseas Vietnamese living in Cambodia for a long time. I and my mother have lived in a village together with my mixed-blood Cambodian husband for four years. While he's drunk, he hits and tortures me so hard. My mother witnesses my agonies, so she wants us to flee to Vietnam. Although we have no cousin here. And waiting he fell asleep after drinking, we rowed the junk to the confluence and then it sank.

Listening to her story, monk Nam Khien understood that he was going to face a hard time.

The young woman kept silent for a while then sobbed. This time these women had no shelter, no relatives that could help them. Nevertheless, his situation here was so difficult. He had no home and must wander on a junk. The young woman cried sadly in the dark corner and said:

-Now we couldn't go to anywhere

Monk Nam Khien said:

-Ms. Nhieu, please calm down, you can stay here. Only move away when you find a cousin somewhere

-Yes, we'd like to say thank you so much

Nhieu got inside and talked to her old mother. Now monk Nam Khien didn't find a way to earn his life when two more strange people arrived at the islet.

The next afternoon, while the monk was bringing firewood to the cabin from the junk, he suddenly stopped when a big, dark man rowed his boat to the islet bank. The stranger pointed a finger at Nhieu's junk nearby and then yelled loudly:
-Give back my wife. F …. king woman, she stoles it from me

He handled a machete and walked quickly toward the cabin. Nhieu just exposed her head outside to watch. When she saw her ex-husband, she got back immediately. Monk Nam Khien moved ahead to stop him:
-You should go home. Nhieu has been beaten and tortured, so she left you now.
-She's my wife, I'm her husband. Who are you?
Monk Nam Khien calmly explained:
-Nhieu was given birth by her parents, so her body did not belong to you. Now her heart doesn't love you

anymore, then she's not your wife. A strong man who hit a woman is a coward

The strange man said angrily:

-F ... king man, step away. I'll chop you at once

No more warning, the man wielded the machete in his hand and chopped towards his rival's head. The monk is standing motionless, brandishing tree logs to defend himself. The wild scream of the stranger man sounded loudly over the quiet river. He's too cruel and strong, so monk Nam Khien had to withdraw step by step. Suddenly, Nhieu jumped down from the cabin door. Armed with a log, she angrily hit the head and flank of her ex-husband with a fierce voice:

-Son Hong, I'll kill you

Monk Nam Khien was surprised and stood still, watching Nhieu as cruel as a tiger fought fiercely. Seeing the monk's still motionless, she yelled:

-Brother Nam, give me a hand

Monk Nam Khien got alert, swung the logs, and stroked to the forelegs, and knees of the Cambodian man several times and knocked him down. Nhieu hit his right arm, which made him drop the machete. The monk stopped either, watched his rival sitting on the ground then said:

-You must go now. Nhieu didn't love you anymore

Nhieu's still angry, handed log to defend. Son Hon picked up the machete then walked towards the bank and rowed away. Saw the bleeding arms of monk Nam Khien, she cried:

-Brother Nam, your arms were wounded, let's get inside the cabin, I'll take care of them

Expected that everything shall be calm in the islet. But the next morning, the Cambodian man came back with two other men in a boat. The monk working in the field, when realized the danger, he didn't know how to cope with three angry men. Suddenly, Nhieu cried loudly from the cabin:

-Brother Nam, they come and fight us again

Without fear, she handled a machete and stepped down, standing by Nam Khien. Nhieu yelled:
-Come here, I'm not afraid of you

The junk moved next to the river bank. Son Hon and his men armed with machetes and sticks walked nearer. Right at this moment, Ba Moi and his wife just rowed their junk from a canal. Saw some strangers in the islet, he then asked:
-What's wrong with you, brother Nam?

On the islet, monk Nam Khien's brandishing his hoe to defend himself against the machete. So, he didn't reply. Nearby, Nhieu couldn't fight back Son Hong's men. She was hit on the shoulder by a stick. Jumped from his junk, Ba Moi handled a pole then ran fastly to the scene and screamed fiercely as thunder. He hit hard to the face of the cruelest man and took him down. By the way, his pole thrusted to the throat of the other. This wounded man ran to the bank. His wife handled the machete and joined the fight. She helped the monk against Son Hong.

After knocking down two enemies, Ba Moi's voice sounded loudly to his wife:
-You come and take care of Miss Nhieu

Ba Moi used his pole as skilled as a club to strike Son Hong badly. He's so afraid then drops his weapon, and flees after his men. The trio jumped into their junk and quickly rowed towards the river that flows across the border.

Heard the bad news from Ba Moi who just come back to the village, right in the mid-noon Sau Tung brothers rowed their junk to see monk Nam Khien. Bay Tung said:
-Brother Nam, if you feel not safe here, let's bring all people to the village
-Thank you. Now they knew the villagers living nearby. Maybe they won't come back again
Sau Tung hung a piece of bomb fragment to a beam under the roof:
-You can strike this metal piece to warn us if they come again

-Thank you

oOo

Nam Khien brought back more logs and nipa palm leaves to the islet. He expanded the cabin with the Sau Tung brothers' help.

The first potato crop was done. Now it's time to prepare land for next season. Nhieu looked after her blind mother, then helped Nam Khien in the field and cared for the vegetable garden. The sweet potato vines quickly grew up and covered almost the islet.

Then in a later afternoon, two rangers drove a motor boat to see the monk. The brown thin elder man asked:
-Are you Nam Khien?
-Yes, I am
-It's illegal to live here. This land belongs to the local authority, so you have to move out at once monk Nam Khien replied:
-I built the cabin here last year

The ranger insisted:

-No, this is an order from province authority, that you must leave. A watching post will be built in this confluence.

Monk Nam Khien kept silent. He understood it was in vain to beg. He patiently saw Nhieu standing by the threshold with anxiety in her face. After the rangers had left, Nhieu stepped nearer and asked:

-Brother Nam, what did they say?

-They will build a post here and ask us to leave

-Where do we go now?

The monk calmly replied:

-It doesn't matter. Must not worry about this ... Any way we move to Sau Tung's village in the canal

The next day, the local ranger team sent their men to the islet. The monk shelter now becomes a watching post.

A week later, in the sunset, while three rangers were drinking local spirits in the post, someone opened fire through the cabin wall from the confluence across the border. Two rangers were seriously wounded. Their alarm resounded in the dark. In the floating village, many men stayed tranquil and kept drinking. They heard the motor boat was moving fast to the town downstream.

The next morning, other rangers came to Sau Tung village to investigate the gunfire. People said that Son Hon or contraband men took revenge. According to the local authority's comment, the remnants of Khmer Rouge guerillas hid from nowhere across the border and fired their weapons. Though the war ended several years ago.

oOo

Then the rainy season came back. The wild swamps and rivers near the border were flooded again. Monk Nam Khien and local villagers daily rowed to fish, and pick up vegetables, and firewood as before. They often rowed across the post sitting in the islet with silence.

Nhieu now was a housekeeper. She cooked and cared for her old mother and Monk Nam Khien's home. She and other women daily rowed into swamp fields to pick vegetables, set fish traps...

In October, a big flood submerged the high ground and spilled over the village. The borderland now turned into a vast lake. From every corner of the delta, strong thick brown silt current swept everything out to big rivers.

A huge flood rushed to the confluence mixing with cruel whirling winds that swept the ranger post away in a stormy day. Two men were staying in the cabin and luckily escaped in a motorboat.

When the bright dry season came back, the river slowly dried up. The villagers couldn't see the islet sat by the confluence as before. The flooding current swept it away and left no remnant behind.

The wilderness of the swamps now restoring its tranquility under the blue clear sky of the summer./.

THE THIEF FROM "THAT SON" MOUNTAINS

Manh's house sat alone in a shallow valley on Mount Cam, within That Son range rising in the western Mekong delta near the Cambodia border. This mountainous area was surrounded by vast tropical forests overwhelming with mysterious stories. Among the tranquil wilderness, small trails were weaving through valleys, gardens, and fields of mountainous villages. Following these trails up higher, amidst the green landscape, people could see small huts, temples, or pagodas hidden in the silence of nature.

Manh, a young man, has lived in this area for nearly two years. Once a week or ten days, Manh returned old home in a hamlet near rice fields by the foothill. Sometimes he didn't like to go up and down the steep, bumpy roads, he stayed in the valley for a whole month.

Manh's day passed peacefully like clouds flying slowly across the sky. He's often in the fields from morning till dusk. On other days, he went to the forest to set some traps or picked vegetables and bamboo shoots then sell in the local market.

All year round, just a few strangers appeared in this remote hamlet. They were people of the local commune, where Manh's family has been living, went up to the valley to bring crops back home, or saw their cousin and visited some temples. People in the village at the foothill, mostly like to sit at the office just talking and drinking. They came here a few times a year to check the wood fire situation.

Manh's nearby neighbor was Mr. Chin Tham, who was also a farmer. He came here to clear land during wartime to grow potatoes and other crops. Walking two kilometers further through the forest to a rocky slope was Mr. Sau Ngung's hut. He was about 50 - 55 years old, a silent monk who was a martial arts master, having roots in the Vietnam - Cambodia border, and was living in this region for years. People in this area have told the rumor that he had been an infamous robber, smuggler in That Son mountain and along the Vinh Te canal. And more than 10 years ago, for unknown reasons, he quit a bad job, then left his wife and children. Mr. Sau Ngung began a new life here as a frugal monk.

Manh often came to visit Mr. Sau Ngung – that local people often called him the monk. Seeing Manh as a gentle neighbor, the monk has accepted him as his disciple. From then, Mr. Sau Ngung began teaching him the martial arts that originated in central Vietnam.

Last month, Mr. Sau told Manh the stories about his past years as a boss of a robbery band and smugglers operating along the Hau River, spreading to Cambodia land and on the canal from Chau Doc to Ha Tien province. At present, he revealed that he has quit already. But, he sometimes went down the mountain at night to break into the homes of some rich bad men to help poor people. Watching Manh with calm eyes, he suggested if Manh wanted to do good things, he could join. He silently thought about the monk's invitation. For people in the western region by That Son mountains, being taught martial arts or literature without condition was a favor. Now, joins with the monk to steal money from bad people, according to Manh, there wasn't a crime. Manh nodded.

From that day on, Manh secretly went down the mountain with Mr. Sau Ngung to make some break-in the neighboring commune. The two victims were retired taxmen of the district. Their house appears normal outside to avoid being noticed. But people in the town market said they were very rich. Mr. Sau Ngung often listened and gathered the rumors when he brought vegetables and fruits down the mountain to trade for money before making a decision.

In two broke-in cases, Manh witnessed the monk's skillful movements when he got into the house through the upstairs window in the dark. Two tax men lost money but weren't walking to the police station. Therefore, nobody in the town market at the foothill knew anything about the burglary.

Three weeks later, Mr. Sau showed some money and told him silently visit two small pagodas in Chau Doc, and make donations. So, they could feed orphans and wandering elderly people. He also told Manh to see if anyone in the village was poor, let's give them rice, not money. Because doing so will easily attract the neighbors' attention.

oOo

The mid-dry season is now in February. But morning in the Mount Cam, the air was cooler and milder than in the Mekong Delta. In the field, Manh used a small hoe to deepen a trench to bring water from a nearby stream into the middle of the garden to irrigate corn and okra plants. On the top of the mountains, a large white mist layer floats over the dark green forest. From afar, Mr. Chin Tham was walking on the trail winding through the potato and bean beds. The neighbor got closer, Manh stopped working and asked:

-Where are you going so early in the morning, Uncle Chin?

-If you still have rice, lend me some. The day after tomorrow, when I go down to the village, I'll buy some more and send back to you

-Yes. You could return it whenever you have

He looked the freshwater flowing into the field and said:

-The cornfields here are so good. Last year, did the wild birds come and loot them? Mine, I have to watch the wild parrots all-day

Manh nodded and said:

-Same with you

The two walked back to the house under the shade of bamboo trees. Manh went in scooped up a few rice cans and poured them into a small plastic bucket. He gave it to the neighbor:

-Here's rice, Uncle Chin

-I'm going home the day after tomorrow, do you want some more stuff? I'd buy it for you

He replied:

-No, thank you. I'll go back village next week

Standing on the porch, Mr. Chin asked:

-You're still learning martial arts with Mr. Sau Ngung in the afternoon?

Manh replied:

-Yes, during the day, he is busy in the garden or sometimes in the woods. Just free in the evening

Mr. Chin said:

-I don't see him coming down here for a few weeks. Is he well?

-Mr. Sau Ngung is fine

- Oh, I'd go down the foothill. If my dog stray here, please give it something to eat

-Yes, I do

The neighbor carried the bucket and walked away along the trail. Manh returned to the fields. The valley was quiet in the morning. Somewhere in the wood, the birds chirping from the tall canopy then quickly vanished into the vast still space.

In the evening, after dinner, Manh walked up to the hut of Mr. Sau Ngung. The martial arts master was sweeping dead leaves on the yard surrounded by rocks and trees. From here, Manh could see the foothills and houses by rice fields, and trees sinking into the shadow when the sunset. The martial arts master was a quiet man. After work was done, he stepped into the hut to light the oil lamp. Out here, Manh practices martial arts alone following the particular ways to build arms and legs as hard as steel that Mr. Sau Ngung passed down. Firstly, he had to move up and down the trails on steep mountain slopes. Then he learned the strange martial arts positions. These main moves were used to evade the rival's blows. Mr. Sau Ngung always warned him to avoid unnecessary fights. Just using martial arts for self-defense or sometimes to help others. That's when life is threatened or defend the weak one.

Right in that evening, he and the monk broke-in the cooperative store of the district in the foothill. They took a small amount of money from the locker and quietly disappeared into the dark.

The next day, at late noon, Manh went down to the village and had a coffee. He heard people in the shop say, that the police just come in the morning to investigate last night's theft. They didn't suspect anyone yet.

Two days later, while he was digging in the potato field, Mr. Chin Tham sent the rice back and said:
-The district trading store was broken-in, and money in the cupboard was taken. The district officers sent an investigation team, but the culprit was still unknown
Manh pretended not to know anything:
-That's it, Uncle Chin!
-Yes, they said nothing. I returned the rice I had borrowed the other day
He put down the hoe and handled the bucket from the neighbor's hand:

-Give it to me... I'm about to have a break. I'd try to hoe a little more then go back to cooking

Mr. Chin Tham joyfully said:

- Thoi came back from Saigon. He asked, how you are

Manh laughed:

-I heard he has got a job as a security guard.

-Yes, he asked a relative there to lead him in searching for work. Thoi said farming here could not make money. Then for a long time, he plans to learn to repair his motorbike or become a van driver when he has got a stable job. He said next time, he will stay longer and come up here to visit you

oOo

Manh imagined that life in this remote village would forever revolve around rice fields, potatoes, and corn gardens like in past times. But a few years later, the poor countryside around That Son range gradually changed. Travel tours take visitors from Saigon, Can Tho, My Tho, and everywhere to visit pagodas, temples, and beautiful scenes of the mysterious, green lush mountains of That Son. Shops, hotels, and motels grew from the foothills to the forests and lakes above the hillsides. Smelling the money and wealth, merchants, mobs, and thieves... fiercely flocked to do business like floods pouring into the western Mekong delta yearly.

Some people came to find Mr. Sau Ngung. They proposed a cooperative plan to build a large temple surrounded by shops, restaurants, and motels. But the quiet monk had refused. Manh's remote hamlet either, cannot escape the business fever that overwhelming around Mount Cam. Seeing the beautiful valley view, town people came to meet him with bunches of money and suggested buying his family land. But they were farmers who loved the land. So his father shook his head. Undeterred, some traders then offered a much bigger money bunch. But they couldn't win the love of the land of local farmers.

Inspired by the new waves, young people in the village quit farming. They borrowed some money to buy a motorbike. Young farmers now rode passengers back and forth across the roads of That Son mountain for money. Poor men like Manh, have to work as porters to carry goods from the foothill to the motels, shops, and restaurants sat on Mount Cam in their free time. Some evening when he got home, it was quite late. After cooking dinner, Manh went to the monk's hut. In the dark, he talked or practiced a few martial arts moves with Mr. Sau Ngung. Being trained on steep rocky slopes for years, Manh could withstand the hard work of a foot transporter on the long mountain roads.

The rumors of good and easy money business lured scammers, fortune tellers, loan sharks, and gangsters to dwell around That Son area.

Mr. Sau still lived peacefully in his remote hut. A few times a month, he carried vegetables to the commune market to sell or trade for other stuff. Sometimes on the way back from the market, he had a drink to refresh at a coffee shop or rode on a motorbike back seat to the hut. In the eyes of local people, Mr. Sau was just a poor and gentle monk.

One time, while sitting in a roadside shop, witnessing the poor shop owner being assaulted by two mobsters who came to collect debt. Got the discontented feeling, he stood up to stop them. Unexpectedly, he was pushed down by one of these bad guys. But Mr. Sau calmly went back to his seat in the corner. Manh was passing by with a heavy load, and the loud noise from the coffee shop stopped him. He went to the monk's place and asked a few questions. The monk said he was fine. The two bad men sent some vulgar words to the shop owner before running away. Manh said goodbye to Mr. Sau Ngung, then went down the foothill to carry goods up to an inn.

Next week, the big house built with a solid gate and reinforced door belonging to a loan boss was intruded on by a thief in mid-night. As rumors, all his money was taken away.

As a prominent body in the gang of mobsters, he did not report to the local police station. His house being filtered and stolen driving him mad. The day after, he immediately sent his vassals to find out the burglars who dared to challenge him. Traders, motorbike drivers, porters, and other mobsters laughed and spread rumors throughout Mount Cam. But the thief's identity and name were still unknown.

oOo

Every day, Manh both working in the field and as a porter went up and down the mountain to earn money. In the evening, when darkness was covering the valley, he went to the monk's hut to learn martial arts and then left without any regular schedule.

Almost every night, he often recalled the night the monk and he broke into the house of the loan boss near the foothill. His big house was built in the middle of a lush garden surrounded by a high wall. Behind it, there was a large buffalo barn guarded by fierce dogs. Getting close to the wall, the monk threw some pieces of buffalo meat laced with drug into the yard to neutralized his two cruel dogs. Waiting about fifteen minutes, the two climbed into the darken yard and waited for some more time. Mr. Sau put his bag on his shoulder and told Manh to go first. They moved to the buffalo barn that was roofed by thick thatched and straw. Then he climbed up and hid in the straw ball under the thatched roof. At noon the next day, waited for the loan boss and his wife and children to take a nap in downstairs rooms. After giving another buffalo meat to the dogs, Mr. Sau, like a ghost, sneaked through the half-closed back door and went upstairs then hid in the corner of the closet. Patiently waiting until midnight, the martial arts master moved to the main room. Knowing that the whole family was asleep, he calmly opened the big cupboard, collected money and gold bracelets, then went downstairs and left.

Two months later, the fresh rains of the season fell on That Son range. The travel business dropped to a low level when people gradually ceased to visit. One weekend night, Mr. Sau Ngung and Manh broke into the home of a hotel owner near the top of the mountain. This rich man had been a border customs officer, now he left and ran his own business, and his wife was staff of a trading company in Chau Doc town. After retiring, he bought land, and then built shops and motels to launder dirty money.

During the off-season, the large motel turns off the lights early. The owner and his wife slept in a two-story house and sat in the backyard. All rooms were shielded by steel doors. Mr. Sau knew he couldn't break through these solid doors, so he climbed onto the roof from a tall tree growing behind the house. From there, the monk got inside through the ventilation hole on the upper floor. About ten minutes later, a rope was dropped for Manh to climb on. In the dark room, after staying motionless for some moment, he saw the couple soundly asleep like the dead. The monk used a small crowbar to prise the hard cupboard and to get money and gold bars inside. The two silently retreated out the same way.

A few days after the break-in at the motel, Manh was hired to carry goods to a restaurant at the top. After delivering to the owner, he and two other young men took a rest under trees shade. Nearby, three motorbike drivers were loudly joking about the thief's intrusion into the rich man's motel. This time, the police launched a thoughtful investigation to detect the burglary around the area.

The suspects were motorbike drivers, mobsters, vendors, and porters that daily moved up and down the mountain roads. But nobody has been arrested till now.

oOo

Every year, when the Lunar New Year comes, the weather on Mount Cam gets cooler and more beautiful. Tourists eagerly joined local festivals and strolled on the lush green mountain trails of That Son region.

Manh closed the door and left the house in the mountain then went back to the old one in the foothill. The next day, he met Thoi, a neighbor, and a close friend just come from Saigon to visit his family. Seeing each other after a long time, Thoi invited Manh to a coffee shop and sat on the road wound up the mountain. Everywhere people and vehicles moving in cheerful and noisy air. Manh's old classmate has now almost changed from the dress and speech of a city man. Thoi ordered two iced coffee cups and asked:

-How are you? Last time I came back just a few days, so I didn't have time to go up there

-Yes, it's fine over there. I'd heard your dad talk to me. Will you stay for a long time after the new year?

Thoi took out a cigarette pack and put it on the table. Outside, the traffic was crowded with local people and travelers moving up and down. Amidst the noisy sounds, Thoi replied:

-About ten days and then I had to go back to Saigon. Likely, this new year is funnier than the last.

-Yes, people love to see the mountainous scenes and pay a visit to pagodas, temples

-Probably you right – Thoi nodded

Manh asked:

-It's easy to get a job in Saigon?

-I had to beg my uncle's aid to apply as a security guard for a company. I'm living in his house. Now after work, I have enrolled in a driving school and am trying to get a driving license. Maybe next year, I will change to another job. Was the crop good this year?

-It's quite good. When I have free time, I carry goods up and down for owners to earn money. Tomorrow let's go to the mountains. There are restaurants, and shops up there

Thoi smiled:

-There are a lot of people in our hometown who eagerly do business and get rich. Do you still learn martial arts with Mr. Sau Ngung, the monk?

Manh replied:

-Yes. Before the new year, he went down the mountain to visit a relative in the town and asked me to watch over his house

-My father saw him walking with a stick to take a motorbike to Chau Doc. He's so good, everyone in this village loves him

-Yes, three days ago, he climbed up a rocky trail to pick medicine plants and vegetables. Unfortunately, his left foot was wounded by a cut

Many local villagers forgot New Year's time They tried making money when tourists from all over corners came to That Son to enjoy festivals. A few motorbike drivers near their homes quickly passed by on the road. A man on a Honda bike, together with a disabled middle-aged man in the back seat, holding a guitar just stopped. Thoi asked:

-Uncle Nam and Mr. Hau riding up to the mountain? Have some coffee then leave

The disabled man asked:

-You and Manh, how long have been here?

-Not so long. You do not enjoy the new year - Manh said

oOo

The motorbiker laughed:

-Oh no, there are many people over there. We would sing at the temple to earn some money

Hau, the disabled man said:

-Now we go up there

-Yes

They disappeared into the middle of crowded pedestrians. Manh was smoking a cigarette when two girls passed by with new clothes. Saw him and Thoi in the coffee shop, and both of them immediately stopped:

-Hello Manh and Thoi, do you want to escort us to the mountain?

Thoi looked at him and smiled. Manh said:

-Yes, let's go. But wait a moment, I pay for coffee

He and Thoi left the shop. Two youngsters and two nice girls followed the crowd walking under the tree's shade along the road. Their laughs burst into noisy air.

oOo

In early April, Mr. Chin Tham went down to the village at the foothill for two days and then returned to the mountain to meet Manh. He said:

- Thoi called back home from Saigon. He has asked for a job at a construction site near him. If you agree, go back to the village and call him

-I'll be back tomorrow. Did he say anything else?

Mr. Chin gave him a piece of paper and replied:

-No. Here's his phone number. He just said you ought to go there. After that, his friends will recommend a place where you can learn to be a mechanic. You can live with him at the same house in District 4

Manh was happy and felt secure. He knew Thoi had a good plan for him.

Manh returned home at the foothills and then called Thoi in Saigon. After fulfilling the task for the next trip, he went back to the valley and said goodbye to Mr. Sau Ngung. Knowing that young people like Manh were lured by Saigon, a noisy big city, Mr. Sau Ngung wished him a successful departure and advised him to stay healthy. The martial arts master gave him some money to spend on his needs.

Saigon was a megacity with millions of people. Manh was amazed while riding in the streets always full of noise, dusty vehicles, and bikes, and crowded with people and shops.

Manh's job was as a security man at a construction site sitting in an old area that had been demolished then building a new high office and supermarket tower. The construction site's back gate was opposite the building where Thoi was being a gateman. Manh just crossed the intersection and made a brief walk under tree shades within a few minutes to see Thoi.

When Thoi led Manh to see the chief of the site. He said, the old guard was sick and had to leave for a while. The boss urgently needed a new man to watch the construction site at night. Seeing him young, strong build, of course, he nodded his head. Just questioned Manh more about home and family to consider if he can trust him. Thoi secured his job by introducing himself as a gate man of the nearby building across the street. Then verified Manh was his neighbor in the hometown. Good luck, when the chief of the site learned that he was a martial arts boxer, he again nodded.

The work here was not too hard. During the day, Manh and a middle-aged security man sat next to the main gate to check the strangers, vehicles carrying materials, and other things that went in and out of the site. The back gate only opened when workers to cleaning up garbage or the front gate was jammed by hard traffic.

In the evening, staying alone, Manh closed the gates and turned on the lights. During the nightfall, he woke up several times to patrol along the site fence to guard against the thief.

The first week, Manh felt quite tired. He just moved around the construction site. But Thoi often saw him almost every afternoon. They were smoking and talking until evening. Manh felt comfortable when he met Thoi in the quiet air of Saigon.

After ten days, in the evening Manh locked the gates. He and Thoi went to a nearby coffee store. Here they could watch Saigon people, listening to the noisy traffic in the street. The bustling life here was different from the boring atmosphere in the countryside. Many new things in a big city made him surprised. Thoi said, that about a kilometer away from a construction site, there was a vocational school. Manh could attend some training courses to get the mechanic license in the evening. According to Thoi, Manh could walk there because it's not very far. Manh was happy. He hoped to have time to enroll in some courses as he had planned.

oOo

In four months, the building rose up to the sixth floor. When Manh came here, the workers began building the heavy foundation, then went to the first floor. The site was very noisy from morning till evening.

In Saigon, he has learned new things that countryside peasants often talk and chat about when they have drinks in coffee shops. Their stories spin around rich men, nice houses, and fancy cars in Saigon. After ten years, when foreign companies doing business, some people suddenly became rich. Luxury shops opened on the boulevards, and hotels and restaurants sat in the downtown. Night clubs, bars signs sparkling in the night.

Those who briefly got rich were businessmen and state officials. They gradually adapted to the Western lifestyle. Owned large houses, driving expensive cars. Enjoyed meals siding by expensive wine bottles, and hi-end foods.

When Thoi was on night shift to guard the nearby building, Manh often walked there after dinner. In the evening, all offices were shut, so the whole building sank in the dark. Right the third time, he noticed a new fancy red car, that often moved in and out the basement after eight o'clock. Sitting behind the wheel was a nice, well-dressed girl. While talking with Thoi about the red car just drove into the street. He asked:

-Is this high-rise top roof inhabited by some people, Thoi?

Time nodded:

-Yes, there is a house over there

-Who's the young girl in the red car?

Thoi whispered:

-The owner of this building made a joint venture with an unknown official in Da Nang. They built it for rent. I heard the rumor, that she was mistress of that big fish. At night, she often went to bars until midnight. Actually, in a few months, she would travel with him somewhere. They only returned to Saigon after a long week holidays.

Manh said:

-That girl has a beautiful car

The weather is changing. Frequent rains fell on Saigon, making trees gain back their lush green again after the dry harsh season. At night, he went to the top floor of the construction site to look over the rooftop of the building across the street. Hidden by the thick foliage of tall trees that grow on the sidewalks, Manh could only watch the flowerpots and a corner of the tiled roof protruding from the dark.

The next day in the afternoon, after the last workers had left, Manh closed the site's gates and went up to the old place to watch once more. The girl's house sitting in a corner of the top floor. She was there. The door and windows were opened to the west, where a small garden full of plants and flowers. To the northwards, there was a small door opening over the terrace. Manh guessed, that way down foot stair. By the east was another old four-story building. They said it was a city tenement house. After long years, the flat owners there have changed drastically. Now, in the building, there were all kinds of people, including workers, students, vendors, and some girls working in restaurants, and bars.

Manh built a plan to break into the girl's house. He went down to the ground floor and turned on the lights around the site. Sitting in the quiet gateman's room, Manh estimated the distance from the present floor of the site to the big branch of the tree on the sidewalk. Then he thoughtfully calculated the gap between two tree lines on both sidewalks. For sure, he turned back to the top floor and watched again. The veranda light illuminated the bench where the girl was playing with her cat. The large branch of an old tree across the street was reaching the iron balcony of the building. Manh carefully estimated a safe way that evade the risk of falling. He thought a man could break into the girl's house if he could overcome the space between two old trees growing opposite on the sidewalk. Looking down from above, the small road was deserted during the day, it had fewer passersby at night. A few homeless people wandered back and forth under the dim yellow light and then disappeared.

The next midnight, the clock on the wall of the gateman's room showed noon. After making a full patrol around the site, Manh went up to the fifth floor, handed the rope of the construction site, and tied it to an iron hook. He threw the rope that hooking to a large branch, so it could cling tightly there. Trying to pull back a few times to ensure that it was safe. Then he tied the other rope end to a concrete pillar and slowly moved out to the tree. When getting there, he sat on a branch and rested for a while. Wait for the fear to go away, and he carefully moves back. Thanks to the days of practicing on the rocky slopes around the monk's hut, Manh overcame this hard distance quite easily.

Next time he brought another rope and hung it over his shoulder. Swinging over the branch, he tied the rope around the sturdy branch as per the monk's instruction. Then remove the iron hook and slowly swing back to the building. He pulled the anchor rope, then the knot was loosened, and retrieved it.

That night, sitting in the calm air under the night sky, he learned how to cross the gap between two old trees on the sidewalk. It was the most dangerous stage before reaching the terrace.

Finally, after nights of silently practicing with daring mind, Manh reached the rooftop of the building across the street. It was past midnight, looking around and seeing only still darkness, he gently moved around the girl's house.

Recalling Thoi said, no one could get to this highest floor without the key of the door leading to the hallway.

From there, the door opened to the terrace. Manh watched the main door. It was armored and fitted with a Japanese anti-theft smart lock.

Manh looked, and tried memorizing the positions of door, windows, and left. When he was swinging from the branch to the fifth floor of the construction site, the wind suddenly blew loudly, the canopies shook violently. Manh feared that the wing was going to throw him down to the sidewalk. Then the rain poured down in torrents, leaving him soaked and shivering in turbulent air. Too risky to wait the rain went away, Manh held tightly to the rope, swinging through the rain and strong wind. Successfully turning back, he panting and looked at the fearful darkness around him. Across the street, the girl's house was sinking under violent currents pouring down from heavy clouds.

By August, workers had finished the last concrete floor. The contractor was now urged by the boss to hurry the remaining works early so that the building could be inaugurated and greet the client. The boss announced that workers could have evening shifts to ramp up the construction pace. The building must be quickly handed over before the opening date in mid-September or earlier. This news made Manh felt a bit worried. He was waiting for a chance when the girl to leave the city for a few days.

He often met Thoi in the evening to study the situation. Evening just falling, the girl still sat behind the wheel of the fancy car, whether the weather was rainy or windy or dry.

At night, Manh stood on the fifth floor of the construction site, looking at the girl's house on the rooftop. Sometimes the lights were turned on when she had just returned from somewhere at midnight. Down on the street, homeless men carrying trash bags on their shoulders, gather the remains in two large bins near the back gate of the building. Every day at dawn, cleaning trucks will come and wash up trash on both sidewalks.

It's past midnight, the city downtown lights still shining as if waiting for dawn. Another day is coming from the east. Manh went down the stairs, walked to his room, and lay down to sleep.

At the beginning of September, Manh's long-awaited opportunity appeared. City residents have some days off on major holidays. Vehicles gradually disappeared on the roads. The noisy atmosphere slowly calmed down. The first night, Manh went up to the fifth floor many times to monitor the dark house of the girl.

The second day, at midnight, he swung over the rope and safely reached the balcony. He sat in the dark and watched. Manh didn't see the girl move out of the building but understood she wasn't there. He easily got inside. The girl didn't close the window. Manh hands a small flashlight to shine around the corners. He found himself in a luxurious kitchen. Nearby was a spacious living room decorated with expensive wooden furniture. Inside the warm bedroom, a large bed and light blue curtains hanging on the walls. The house has some wooden cupboards and an iron safe. Looking inside them, he found cash and US dollars. In another, there was gold jewelry with precious stones. He took it all and put it in his pocket. While checking the safe, a strange noise from the kitchen startled him. Thinking the owner of the house suddenly returned. Manh turned off the light and quickly hid behind the curtain in the room corner. The sound from the old corner echoed in the dark. He laughed and walked over to watch. A white cat with black spots was eating something in a bowl. It looked up at him and meowed a few small sounds. Manh caressing the cat and looking out to the garden.

Maybe the girl didn't close the window, so it freely wandering everywhere. He returned to the bedroom and looked at the safe for a while before deciding not to touch it. Searching two more wooden cub boards in the kitchen and finding just invaluable things, Manh climbed out and closed the window. In the dark yard, plants and flowers gently move their branches and leaves in the cold wind. Guessing the coming rain, Manh swung back to the site.

Hiding all things in a secret place in the wall, then brought the rope back to their usual place. Going down to the bathroom, Manh peeled off the tape that wrapped on his ten fingers, threw them down the drain, and washed thoroughly before going to bed.

Thoi told Manh about the theft two days later when they two met in the afternoon at the construction site. Only the security team got this news from the building manager. They tried hiding the theft to avoid worrying everyone. The police went to the girl's house to watch the traces and proofs. They then questioned the staff on duty during the two-day holiday. It seems that all suspicions point to the nearby old building.

In early October, the building was accomplished. The boss announced that it was time to welcome the first clients.

Manh was accepted by the site chief as a gateman for another project.

The director of the new building also wanted to hire him as a guardsman.

While hesitating, news of big floods spilling from Chau Doc to Kien Giang appeared daily in newspapers in Saigon city. Manh asked the chief a permission to return to his village for half a month. Thoi also left to visit his home. They two went to the coach station to buy tickets and then board a bus back home.

The bus drove by the western gateway of Saigon suburb heading to the Mekong delta. Green rice fields submerging under the clear sunlight sparkling on both sides of the highway.

The car crossing a long bridge over the Vam Co river, Manh looked at the murky brown water filled with silt rolling below it. The scene made him recall the countryside when flooding waters overflowed the banks to the foothill of That Son range. The mountains in the southwest border region appeared dimly in the mist and smoke under heavy rains overwhelmed the sky. The bus runs tirelessly to the southwest. Manh watched the green fields spreading far away to the horizon and dreamed of walking on the Mount Cam trail to his home in the quiet valley./.

THE TOWN WITHOUT COFFEE SHOPS

Vinh arrived at this coastal town in the Mekong River delta on the last bus of the day. Leaving the station, he walked to a small, three-story hotel on a quiet street. After checking in and showering to remove dust and dirt, he went down the stairs and stepped out of the hotel, standing on the sidewalk as evening gradually came down. Vinh turned rightward where dime lights from a few shops shone onto the narrow street. Walking closer, he saw a small eating house, seemingly serving noodles or something like noodles. Feeling hungry, Vinh got in and sat at the innermost table. His eyes touched the man's sight standing behind the cooking stand in the corner. He was likely of Chinese descent, and quickly got

Vinh's order. Looking to the street while waiting, Vinh heard some noises from backward, and then the hot steam of a boiling broth cooker flew around still space. A few minutes later, the man placed a hot bowl of rice noodles on the table shedding thin smoke curling under the light. Vinh bent down, glancing at the ingredients in the bowl. He then added a few red thin chili slices and calmly enjoyed it. Five minutes later, just like as he walked in, Vinh silently stood up and walked out into the street after paying for his meal. The brief conversation between Vinh and the man is just the charge of the noodle bowl. The uneasy feeling of an empty stomach went away. Now Vinh needed some coffee to keep him alert from a long trip to this quiet town from Saigon.

After the war, people in remote towns didn't want to talk to a stranger unless for need. Suspicious air overwhelms city to town and countryside.

Stepping out onto the sidewalk, he thought quickly as late evening down:
-The town is so quiet. It has a coffee shop here?

He looked to both sides of the street, then decided to walk against the wind that blowing from the sea to the inland. Yellow light bulbs hung on the poles shining pale light down to the narrow sidewalk. Few people and vehicles hurried on the street. The wind blowing constantly in the air, he could hear the crashing sounds of sea waves as they were about to submerge the small town. Vinh watched still old houses sit along the sidewalks. He tried to find a coffee shop and had a black coffee cup to stay awake and kill time. Time's still too soon to go back to the hotel. Under the eaves of a house, the light from inside and the street lamp induced Vinh's eyes to three men sitting around a low table. As walking nearer, Vinh saw a small bottle on the table and a dish of dried food. This sign was easy to know, it was a local pub in the countryside of the Mekong Delta. As he passed by, three men, both old and young, were talking loudly. No one paid attention to a stranger on the street.

Near a road junction, several other men were standing and talking. They all turned to look at him and then continued their story. Likely, they were talking about a fishing boat and a captain's name. Vinh stood hesitantly under the veranda. He then decided to walk towards a larger street that stronger winds blowing against him. In a coastal town, a stranger easily attracted everyone here. Even though the war had ended more than ten years ago, fishing men and their boats still secretly departed from somewhere, carrying people to the high sea and then fleeing to other countries. Vinh, he needn't worry about local police checking. He's usually making trips to provinces and doing business with coastal fisheries cooperatives. An official paper with red stamps from a state-owned factory in Saigon was in his wallet. That makes him confidently walk slowly.

At night, in this remote town, Vinh just wanted to find a coffee shop. Some place he'd been before, people needn't wander through streets. Just in front of the inn, people could see a few wooden tables and chairs of a coffee stand on the pavement.

This town sat by the estuary and had an odd atmosphere. He passed several dull streets with shabby poles emitting faint yellow light. That boring scenery evoked the decline and poverty images of visitors. It overwhelmed the old crumbling houses, and tired people walking in the darkness.

The wind still blows strongly from the open sea to inland. There was the cry of a seagull echoing from the night sky. The smell of fish and shrimp and salty mist mixed with the sound of crashing waves in the air. Vinh thought as he walked:
-Maybe the sea market and the pier are ahead, and a coffee shop too

Walking a long way crossing quiet houses shedding dim lights, he saw a few scattered silhouettes of people walking in the same way. Under his feet, a thin sand layer carried by the wind spread to roads in the town. Each time when Vinh's feet moved on it, his sandals likely slid across the road surface, and his body seemed to lose momentum and lean slightly forward. Near the end of the street, he saw an empty local market with a dozen roofed stalls lying haphazardly. Few yellowish dim lights clinging on the poles likely be swallowed into the endless dark of the night overwhelming the sea. On the right side, some men sitting around a table under a light bulb. Vinh guessed they were local fishermen. Gathered below the thatched roof with a spirit bottle and glasses. He had slowly approached. Even saw them drinking spirits, not coffee. The man sitting on his way, turned his head to look. On the other side, the middle-aged man and a youngster seemed paying no attention to him. They were arguing loudly. The middle-aged man with a hoarse voice waved his hand toward quiet boats docking along the wooden pier. Vinh walked over then asked:

- Are you guys waiting to go fishing at night?

A man shook his head and said quickly:

-Tomorrow morning. Now rest and drink some spirits ... Sit down and have a few glasses to heat up

    He spoke with a simple southern accent and pulled out another chair from the darkness towards him. Vinh reluctantly sat next to the table, looking at a half-empty bottle of local spirits and pieces of dried fish in the aluminum pot. The middle-aged man and the young stopped talking and looked at him then smiling politely. One man poured spirits into an empty glass and put it in front of Vinh. Quietness filled the air. They all looked to the darkness at sea. A few moments later, the man sitting near the oldest one asked curiously:

- Did you just come from the city?

Vinh nodded, drank the spirits, then put the glass on the table and replied:

- I just arrived from the city this afternoon. Tomorrow, I'll work with the cooperative office. Then sign a contract to buy shrimps and fish for a city factory. Are you guys belonging to the cooperative's fishing boat team?

Two people across the table swiftly nodded. The man sitting near him poured spirits into a glass and emptied it. His big, rough hands picked up dried fish from the pot, broke it into small pieces, put it in his mouth then chewed. Vinh watched his brown-tanned face and the blue khaki shirt covering his broad shoulders that emerged on his hunchback. He seemed fitting on a fishing boat. He grabbed the bottle and poured spirits into a glass then invited Vinh. The tranquil dark mixing with the yellow lights built a dull asleep air under thatched roofs. On the calm sea, the lights from a lone boat slowly passed and disappeared behind the others anchoring closed together in the cove. Some of them drifted on the waves that crashed to the deserted shore. Vinh emptied his glass, put it down next to the empty bottle, and calmly broke a piece of dried fish. The story of three local men revolved around the last sea trips and the output of other ships in the fleet, and bonuses they just received during Tet. All of them didn't show their upset while night fell quickly. In contrast, they behaved without distance to Vinh's abrupt appearance. The man sitting near him pointed to the empty bottle and said to the youngster:

- Go back to the boat and get some, remember to bring more cigarettes

The young man at the other corner picked up the bottle, stood up, and walked along the cement pier under the twilight light shining the way running towards the boats. He watched two fishermen, neither of them had wrist watch. But Vinh thought no need to worry about the time. He wasn't busy or had to see anyone tonight. These fishermen didn't know that he was looking for some coffee. Without coffee, taking some spirits wasn't harmful anyway. On the other hand, he could learn more news about fishing boats in this town.

The young man returned with two bottles and a pack of cigarettes. The man sitting on the opposite side poured spirits into a glass and said:
- Drink, Mr. Ba

The man wearing the blue khaki shirt tore out a cigarette pack and offered it to him. Vinh pulled out a cigarette, lit it, and took a deep breath. The old one asked the youngster:
- Is there anyone on the boat?
He replied:
- They're all asleep

Everyone drank as the spirit glass moved steadily clockwise on the table. Perhaps they had a lot of time, so the story still revolved around boats and fish. Likely, none of the three fishermen would talk about other stories. Unlike Saigon, people secretly talked about leaving the city by boat trips in the dark defying the danger. The man sitting across the table pointed to the man who wore a khaki shirt and said:

- Mr. Ba is the captain of the biggest boat here

After saying those respective words, he handed up the glass and emptied it. So, the man in the blue shirt was the captain of a cooperative fishing boat. Vinh nodded slightly and tried to watch his rugged dark brown face overexposed under sunlight, his dry and tangled hair soaked by salt water. The cool sea breeze and some glasses of spirits seeping into his veins made his mind went ease. The captain suddenly asked him:

- Your factory is big?

Vinh stopped smoking and replied:

- Very big, we exported goods to Eastern Europe, Russia... Recently, we tried to send products to Singapore and Japan

The young man handled a full glass towards Vinh. While the captain asked about shrimp and fish business in other towns, another man's voice abruptly interrupted:
- Where is the city factory?
Vinh looked at him:
- Binh Chanh, near Long An province. We have bought fish and shrimp from other towns. Can Gio, Tien Giang, Ben Tre, Soc Trang ... They are all located along coastal provinces.

Now the strong spirits smoothly went down his throat. Vinh asked the captain:
-Where will your fishing boat sail to this season?
A brief answer:
-Ca Mau sea
Vinh slowly asked:
-How long for a fishing trip and then back to this pier?

He answered without thinking:

- Four or five days, it depends... If you hit Fish Way, will turn home early

The young man now suddenly talked:

- This season the sea is very calm. Sailing down to Ca Mau, there were a lot of fishing boats, Cambodian boats, and Thai boats too

The man sitting next to him put his naked feet on the chair. His eyes stared at him and the captain then said:

-F...king, the border guardsmen said almost all those boats were pirates

The young man recounted with certainty:

- Yes, their boats had larger engines that easily sped up to chase and rob boat people that crossing the border to overseas. They only feared border guard ships armed with big guns

It seems their story has gone in another way. The captain glared at two local men and ordered them to shut up. The silent air came back. Vinh knew the rules of fishermen in this turbulent time. Boat people's trip usually faces unexpected risks when they sail on the high sea. On the table, there was only a half-empty bottle. Vinh found himself still awake, though his head was a bit dizzy. Vinh's question interrupted the silence:

- There is a coffee shop in this town?

No one answered Vinh. Everyone was smoking. Likely his question fell into an empty room. Three local men were looking at the dark sea in front of them. The middle-aged man across the table put down his red cigarette and said:

-Just a pub serving local spirits

The captain used his hand to wipe across his mouth after drinking and said:

- On the boat, we drink tea, no coffee

Vinh remembered after 1975, Saigon coffee stores suddenly vanished for a while. Some connoisseurs said, if people want to enjoy coffee, they have to keep it secret. Coffee was as illegal and high-end as opium. Some brave coffee shop owners still doing business. They asked clients to wait somewhere. Then they sent someone to lead them to the hidden shop. Customers must drink coffee quickly, pay, and then leave quietly. Contra bands smuggled coffee beans from the Di Linh plateau, Lam Dong through forest trails to Saigon. In recent years, coffee stores have reappeared. But in this coastal town, the drink of magic couldn't be seen anywhere.

Vinh sat with three men until they finished the last spirit bottle. All of them stood up and returned to their hut hidden somewhere in the darkness behind the houses on the right of the pier. The night falling deeper, the wind blowing stronger. The old dog's harsh bark rang out, breaking the silence. Vinh left the deserted beach and turned back to the hotel. He walked slowly step by step on the smooth sand bed of the empty road. Under the yellow light near an intersection, a policeman standing on the sidewalk glanced at Vinh. The small town likely goes to bed early. No one walked around or sat in the street sides.

From the beach, Vinh walked through the hotel door and looked at the clock hanging in the right corner of the wall. Its hands were pointing at almost ten o'clock. Behind the wooden counter, the place where a girl had sat in the afternoon now was a thin, middle-aged man who may be responsible as a security man. The man took the key with the room number and put it on the counter. Saw number seven on the small board card, Vinh took it and walked upstairs. The small hotel just had its steps sound. On the ceiling, some small white fluorescent tubes shined faint pale lights to the old walls.

The next morning, Vinh went down to the hotel canteen. He had breakfast with a bowl of instant noodles with pieces of fresh squid some green vegetables and slices of red pepper. Got out of the hotel, put my bag on my shoulders walked to the fishing port then entered the co-operative's office. He met a man that introduced by a female secretary as a fishing boat manager. Vinh and this man sat and talked in a small quiet room at the far end of the office. Until noon the business deal was fulfilled. Stepping out of his stuffy room with closed windows, Vinh eagerly breathed the fresh outside air. He watched tall poplar trees shade around the office then left.

In the evening, the manager walked to the hotel. He invited Vinh to a small restaurant that sat in a corner of the poplar wood and dunes by the seashore. He seemed familiar with the restaurant owner. A spirits bottle, a big plate of steamed fish, and a plate of boiled squid were served on a wooden table under the shadow of poplar trees whispering in the wind. Vinh and he talked about some more specific details of the business that had been agreed in the morning. Vinh felt things went as good as expected. Joyfully, the manager shows himself satisfied with the new customer from Saigon.

The first contract will last for two months. After emptying up some glass, Vinh showed intention to go on if business would be fine. The local manager smoked and thought a moment, then carefully said:
- This contract must be completed then our cooperative will sign another one

The spirits in the bottle just dropped to a third, but a lot of food on the table. The manager asked the owner to charge and they both left.

Stepping out of the small restaurant, Vinh says goodbye to the man at the corner of the street. Vinh walked through the town center and watched around the street. Some eating houses and stores still serve few clients. On the sidewalk, yellow dim lights shone on a pushing cart selling porridge parked in the empty station of local buses. He walked ahead and suddenly found himself in the middle of a dark street surrounded by sleeping houses. Vinh stood alone, trying to find the way out of an intersection without lights and nobody. Confused and had no idea which way to get out, when seeing a dim light at the end of a narrow road, Vinh decided to move to that side. When he finally reached the intersection, he found a broader road on the left that led to the hotel, just a few hundred meters away.

The next day, a man sailed the boat back into the river mouth. It was hauled to the dry dock to fix the engine and be prepared for a long fishing trip. It took nearly a week for mechanics to check everything in the boat. Then the boat was towed out near the estuary and calmly anchored in a small canal at dusk.

Early the next morning, the boat headed to the big river and docked next to the border guard station. The captain steered it onto a wooden pier. He took the papers to the station to apply for a fishing license. A few minutes later he returned and ordered the sailors to start the engine. The boat sailed down the river through the dark water. The captain stood at the steering wheel while looking at the small town dimly lit in the dark. The boat under his skilled hands calmly moved straight out towards international sea waters.

oOo

By the end of the first contract, Vinh went back to the coastal town by bus. He met the manager of the fishing cooperative in the same room under the shade of a poplar wood. The local man was seemingly so happy when shaking Vinh's hand. Both sides agreed to sign another contract with the same terms as the previous one.

In the evening, Vinh went around the fish market near the sea beach and watched quiet boats docking along the pier. Nobody under empty wooden stalls only strayed dogs and cats living by the market. Vinh didn't go around looking for coffee stores anymore. He just made a stroll after dinner. This quiet coastal town just has pubs to serve local fishermen. The winds blew whizzing over thatched roofs and small flags on the masts then vanished into quiet space inland. Only a few sporadically seagulls dull screams remained behind.

Ten days later a cooperative's second boat sailed to the open sea with more than forty people in the midnight. It moved tirelessly to the sea waters of another country in the southwest of Ca Mau tip. The boat had sailed a peaceful four-day sea journey before docking by a small island. Vinh was a boatman on this lucky trip.

Three years later, Vinh sat on the veranda of a coffee shop on the south coast of Houston, Texas, waiting for a man. He looked at the white-painted boats moored at Kemah wharf and remembered the red-and-blue painted fishing boats in the coastal town on the estuary of a Mekong River branch, Vietnam. Those wooden boats and daring sailors had sailed many Saigon people to the freedom land. His friend, Hoi, who went on the last trip with him, parked the car in front of the shop and walked in. He sat down on the chair and looked at Vinh. Both hands are buried deep in the pockets of the thick coat:

-Texas is so cold this year. Are you missing Vietnamese Tet?

 He smiled and asked:

- Let's have coffee

Hoi nodded./.

Contact author:
Vu Phan
tamkongvu@gmail.com

Contact Publisher
Han Le
han.le3359@gmail.com
(408) 722-5626

www.ingramcontent.com/pod-product-compliance
Lightning Source LLC
LaVergne TN
LVHW091633070526
838199LV00044B/1048